8/19

T

D1394759

UNCLE SHAWN AND BILL

UNCLE SHAWN AND BILL

AND THE NOT ONE TINY BIT LOVEY-DOVEY MOON ADVENTURE

A. L. KENNEDY

ILLUSTRATED BY GEMMA CORRELL

WALKER
BOOKS

This is a work of fiction. Names, characters, places and incidents are either the product of the author's imagination or, if real, used fictitiously. All statements, activities, stunts, descriptions, information and material of any other kind contained herein are included for entertainment purposes only and should not be relied on for accuracy or replicated as they may result in injury.

First published 2019 by Walker Books Ltd
87 Vauxhall Walk, London SE11 5HJ

2 4 6 8 10 9 7 5 3 1

Text © 2019 A. L. Kennedy • Illustrations © 2019 Gemma Correll

The right of A. L. Kennedy and Gemma Correll to be identified as author and illustrator respectively of this work has been asserted by them in accordance with the Copyright, Designs and Patents Act 1988

This book has been typeset in Sabon and Gemma Correll Regular

Printed and bound in Great Britain by CPI Group (UK) Ltd, Croydon CR0 4YY

British Library Cataloguing in Publication Data: a catalogue record for this book is available from the British Library

ISBN 978-1-4063-8626-4

www.walker.co.uk

For V.D.B.

WIGGLING TOES

SECTION ONE

In which everyone is having a lovely time at the beach. And all our friends are definitely not going to have a death-defying, nose-defending adventure really soon.

Badger Bill was lying on the sand at Shoogeldy Bay, which is just below Uncle Shawn's llama farm. He was wiggling his toes in the warm air and letting his fur dry in the last of the day's sunshine. He had been swimming all afternoon, and it was nearly time to go home and have some jam sandwiches and custard and hot chocolate and maybe a few pickled slugs and a banana. Swimming made Bill a bit hungry.

Uncle Shawn had spent the whole spring teaching Bill how to swim and now our badger pal loved running into the waves as fast as his short (but handsome) legs could take him and then swimming about like a plump (but surprisingly graceful) furry fish. As long as he knew that his toes could touch the bottom if he wanted them to, Bill could now happily do the Badger Back Stroke and the Stripey Nose Crawl really quite fast.

CLASSIC BADGER SWIMMING STYLES

① SPINE HELD STRAIGHT

BADGER BACK STROKE

② STRIPEY NOSE CRAWL

NOSE ABOVE WATER LEVEL

③ FRONT VIEW

LOOKS QUITE LIKE A BAT

BADGER BUTTERFLY

④ LLAMA TAIL STROKE

WORKS FOR ANYONE'S TAIL

Carlos and Guinevere Llama were preparing to take their final dip of the day. Carlos and Guinevere didn't know that llamas don't usually swim, so they enjoyed it immensely and could even Llama Paddle all the way out to the sunbathing rock in the middle of the bay. They had also discovered that the beach is a really good place to be if you want to annoy someone, and Carlos always wanted to annoy Guinevere and Guinevere always wanted to annoy Carlos. They loved splashing cold water into each other's ears and putting seaweed into each other's ice creams. Guinevere liked dunking Carlos' towel in rock pools and Carlos liked burying Guinevere's flippers in the sand so that she couldn't find them.

"Carlos, where are my flippers, you sea-weed-smelling llama?"

"It is not my fault if you have lost your swim-ming flippers, you wet and foolish fool."

"Then it will not be my fault if I put sand in your swimming trunks and bite your knees."

CARLOS AND GUINEVERE FIGHTING

If you had listened while Guinevere gripped Carlos' knee between her teeth, you would have heard her mumble, "I do love the beach." Except it would have sounded a bit like, "My moo muv ma meeff." This was because she had her mouth full of llama hair, even though everyone knows you shouldn't speak with your mouth full of anything, never mind llama.

And if you had listened while Carlos kicked Guinevere's leg, you would have heard him mutter, "Why are you saying moo, you silly and annoying llama? Just because you swim like a cow wearing skis, it doesn't mean you have to sound like one." And then he breathed in a big lump of fine sea air and added, "Yes, yes, it is very fine at the beach. It is almost as wonderful as walking up the Alpamayo mountain in Peru. Ouch, ouch, ouch." (That last part was because Guinevere was biting him again.)

Ginalolobrigida Llama was being much more serene and beautiful than her two friends. You cannot be beautiful while you are biting and fighting, so she was lying on her llama beach towel under an umbrella and reading her favourite magazine, *Lives of Luscious Llamas,* and sipping some of the lemonade Bill always made for everyone. She consulted her horoscope, which said, "Soon you will be surrounded by love. You will meet an exciting stranger and perhaps you will find you are wearing jewels." Ginalolobrigida sighed at the thought of how much make-up she could buy with those jewels and how generous she would be after that, maybe buying toys for orphan llamas, because making tiny llamas smile would feel nice.

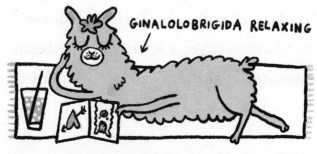

GINALOLOBRIGIDA RELAXING

BRIAN
WORRYING

Meanwhile Brian Llama was sitting under a tree near the beach, because he didn't want to get sunburnt. He was also wearing a thick pullover, in case the weather turned cold suddenly. Brian was worrying that a flying fish might leap out of the sea and slap him on the nose, or that a lobster might walk up and nip him on the nose. He had no safety equipment to defend against fish or lobsters. In fact, Brian was so certain that something terrible was going to happen to his nose that he had wrapped it up in a great big cone of newspaper. This meant he looked like a giant, furry ice-cream cone – woolly-legs-and-pullover flavoured – that someone had dropped on its side under a tree. 🐾

SECTION TWO

*In which – oh no! – something strange begins
to happen. I hope it's not the start of something
horrifying... This section also contains quite
a good joke about polar bears which any
sensible person, or badger, might like.*

Out on the sunbathing rock, Uncle Shawn was
sitting in his favourite, baggiest swimming shorts,
which were patched with bits of old bedspread and
some squares from the kitchen curtains. His wiggly hair and his wiggly ears were hiding under the
floppiest sun hat he could find in his big box of
hats. He was slapping and slathering and slooshing

13

suncream all over his long arms and lanky legs, as if he was a very tall scone that needed buttering.

Once he had buttered his bony, bumpy knees, Uncle Shawn waved with both hands at Bill and sang, very loudly,

"Bill, you have such shiny feet
They are clean and very neat.
All your fur, both black and white,
Shines like fishes in the light.
In pyjamas soon you'll rest
Folded like a tidy vest."

This usually would have made Bill get up and dance his Happy Badger Dance in the sand: *spoof, spoff, spaff.* But Bill didn't seem to be paying any attention. So Uncle Shawn decided to wave both his long arms and his long legs and yell the latest joke he had learned.

"Bill! Bill! Do you know the joke about the father polar bear and the mother polar bear and the little polar bear? They were all sitting on an iceberg in the frozen ocean. Mother Bear said, 'Oooh, I have a tale to tell.' And then Father Bear said, 'Aaaah, I have a tale to tell.' And then Little Polar Bear said, 'Oooww, my tail's told.'" Uncle Shawn waited for Bill to chuckle, or at least smile.

COLD

ASTONISHINGLY COLD

COLDER THAN YOU CAN IMAGINE

But again, Bill didn't even turn his head, never mind roll about on the sand with his paws in the air laughing. This was strange...

CONFUSED UNCLE

DANGEROUS BREEZE →

"Ah, well," sighed Uncle Shawn. "Perhaps my joke was not so very good after all." As he said this, he could see Bill jumping to his feet and then hurrying off out of sight. "I hope it was not such a terrible joke that it would make Bill run away. Hmmm... Maybe the ice-cream van has arrived and he is running to get us ice cream. No, I would have heard the van playing 'This Badger's Gotta Move' on its chimes if it were here... Hmmm..." He sat on the rock and thought and his tummy felt a little bit cloudy.

Still, nothing about Uncle Shawn stayed cloudy for long. He supposed that by the time he got

LLAMA
FIGHT

MYSTERY →

SEAWEED
(FOR THROWING)

RUNNING
BADGER

BURIED FLIPPERS

back to the farmhouse, Bill would be there and would probably have already made cocoa and everything would be happy. The llamas would be rocking in their llama hammocks, or snuggling into their beds of straw and maybe even snoring Peruvian snores, which were called *ronquidos*. The twins, Sam and Sky, would be in their pyjamas. Everyone who was still awake would say goodnight to everyone else and then Uncle Shawn and Bill would watch the sunset together in their matching rocking chairs, set out on the west side of the farmhouse.

Uncle Shawn grinned. "Yes, that will be the

perfect way to end the day. I shall make a big wish so that exactly that will happen." Then he smiled again, because Uncle Shawn's wishes always came true.

At least they usually did...

SCARF IN A WASHING MACHINE

UNCLE SHAWN DIVING

Then Uncle Shawn dived into the sea exactly the way that a nimble otter wouldn't, and splashed about like a scarf in a washing machine – which was just what he wanted to do. 🐾

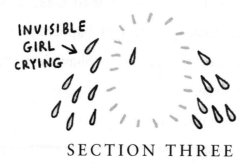

INVISIBLE
GIRL →
CRYING

SECTION THREE

In which we don't find out why Bill didn't pay any attention to Uncle Shawn's nice joke. We need to do something else first. We need to find out why Sam and Sky weren't enjoying the lovely day at the beach.

Sam and Sky, the twins who lived with Uncle Shawn, Bill and the llamas at the farmhouse, hadn't gone to the beach that day, even though they usually really enjoyed it.

Sam had once thought that he might grow up to be a pirate captain, so he loved being near the sea. Sky liked the beach because she could manage to be a bit less invisible there. Before she came to the farmhouse, Sky had wished and wished and wished to turn invisible, so that she could escape from a terrible institution run by an even more terrible man called Sylvester Pearlyclaws. Her wish came true and she had been invisible ever since – even though she didn't want to be any more. At the beach, though, people could see her footprints, and they could watch her making shapes in the sea when she swam and sometimes, just for a moment, her whole outline would be painted all over in sparkly seawater.

Today, however, the twins were curled up together on the big sofa in the farmhouse sitting room and crying. They were both so covered in rolling and falling tears that anyone would have thought the sofa had sprung a leak.

"Oh Sam, I'm making you upset. I'm sorry," snuffled Sky.

"No, no, I was just thinking about onions and vinegar. I'm not crying," sniffled Sam.

"I don't want to be invisible any more," said Sky. "People bump into me as if I don't exist and when I say, 'Hello, let's play,' people think I'm a ghost. And I can't queue for things in the sweet shop because NOBODY KNOWS I AM STANDING THERE AND WOULD REALLY REALLY REALLY LIKE A BAG OF LEMON SHERBET! OOOOOOWWW!"

THE PROBLEMS OF BEING INVISIBLE

① PEOPLE THINK YOU ARE A GHOST

② PEOPLE TREAD ON YOUR TOES

OW

③ BEING VERY BAD AT MIMING (AND CHARADES)

④ SIGH

CAN'T DO SHADOW PUPPETS

"Well, you wished yourself invisible, Sky. Why don't you wish yourself back?"

"I CAN'T! I've tried and tried until my head hurts for weeks. Even wishing as hard as I can, all I get is a ticklish feeling in one foot. I'm going to be stuck like this until I'm an invisible old lady AND I STILL WON'T BE ABLE TO QUEUE UP FOR SHERBET!"

SAD TEACAKES

There was a big dish of teacakes by the sofa, but the twins were so sad that they couldn't eat the tiniest crumb, not so much as a mousenibble.

It almost seemed that whatever made wishes come true had stopped working.

SECTION FOUR

In which we find out why Bill paid no attention to Uncle Shawn's joke. Were Bill's knees so hot that he had to run very fast to cool them? Or had he caught sight of something dangerous and pink...?

Badger Bill hadn't paid attention to Uncle Shawn and his quite-good joke because, over a sand dune, Bill had caught sight of a twirling pink parasol. And then he caught sight of a bright pink bonnet, covered in frills and flounces – and a brighter pink frock, covered in bows and ribbons. And inside all that pinkness? There was a badger – the most beautiful lady badger that Bill had ever seen.

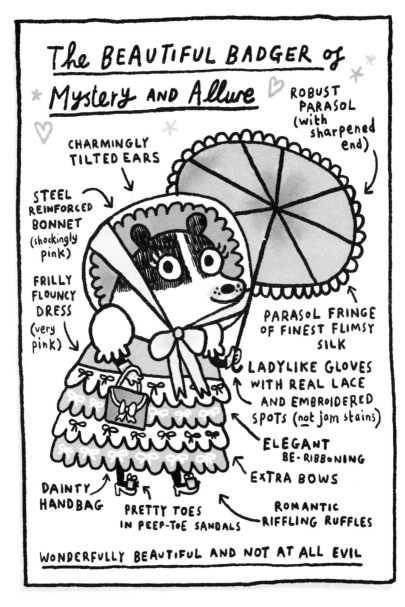

(We won't mention that the only lady badgers Bill had really known up until then were his Aunt Magnolia, who had a wonderful moustache, his teacher Miss Bristlethistle, who was a bit scary, and his mum, who was called Flossie and wasn't scary at all.)

Bill stood up and watched this amazing badger skip over the sand, as if she weighed no more than the tiniest feather from the most romantic bird in the world.

"Oh, my goodness," thought Bill. "She must be a princess, or maybe a long-distance bus driver."

Bill thought being a long-distance bus driver was one of the most wonderful and daring jobs a badger could have – almost as wonderful as being an explorer. Bill wanted to be the greatest badger explorer in the history of badgers going shopping and getting lost and then accidentally discovering entire new continents and volcanoes. He wanted to be the first badger to speak to a Milky

Moon Moth. (Milky Moon Moths are very hard to see and extremely shy – even though they are extremely big – and almost no one has ever spoken to one.)

Meanwhile, Bill's heart was turning cartwheels in his chest and his knees were tingly. Anyone else who felt like that might have rushed to a doctor in case they were very ill, but Bill knew he wasn't poorly – he was in love.

HANDY GUIDE:
HOW TO SPOT THAT A BADGER IS IN LOVE

RINGING IN EARS

STARS IN EYES

HEART TURNING CARTWHEELS

HAPPY NOSE FUR

SINGING IN ELBOWS

PULSE THUMPING LIKE AN ELEPHANT TRYING TO DANCE

KNEES ARE TINGLY

As Bill watched, the lovely lady badger bent down and offered a seagull some crumbs from a dainty sandwich she held in her delicate paw.

"Oh, that proves she's kind as well as the loveliest badger on Earth. Oh, oh, oh, I must go and talk to her before she skips back to whatever marvellous place she came from."

Bill brushed the sand from his fur but was too in love to pick up his backpack or find his water bottle with the picture of Claudia Badger on it. (Claudia Badger had invented edible shoes for emergencies. They were terrible shoes, but made delicious pies if you filled them with filling instead of feet.) None of that mattered – he just needed to speak to HER. He didn't know HER name yet, but it was bound to be something delicate and wonderful, like Mimsy, or Twinklebiscuits.

Bill's pulse was thumping like an elephant trying to tap dance. He closed his eyes so that he could calm down.

In fact, no one was looking at the mysterious badger just then. Carlos and Guinevere were far too busy fighting. Ginalolobrigida was reading. Brian's newspaper nose cone had blown off and he was chasing it – very carefully. And there was a big sand dune between Uncle Shawn and possibly the most gorgeous badger in the world. None of them saw the new badger, and it would have been so useful if they had. It would have been so very useful if they had seen her swimming mysteriously out to the sunbathing rock the night before and then whispering to someone and then swimming secretly back to shore again, punching harmless tiny fish as she went. It would have been even more useful if they had seen her reading a dirty, crumpled piece of paper the day before that – a piece of paper that looked very like a list of really terrible things that a terrible badger might want to do... But no one had seen any of that, not even one tiny suspicious bit of it. 🐾

← INNOCENT SQUIRREL

SECTION FIVE

In which we learn that not all badgers are nice. In fact some badgers are about as horrible as they can get without standing on a ladder to make them seem bigger so they'll have more room for wickedness.

The badger in the pink bonnet was called Miranda, not Twinklebiscuits. And, if anyone had been able to watch her at that moment, they would have seen that she wasn't as wonderful as Bill thought.

Miranda had been feeding crumbs from her sandwich to a seagull, but only so that she could get the poor bird near enough to try to punch it!

While the surprised seagull dodged away, Miranda ate the whole sandwich in one mouthful, stuffing it into her face with both paws. Then she burped a big burp and kicked sand at a young squirrel called Don who was lying on his beach towel reading a comic and doing no one any harm.

Then Miranda Badger laughed with her sandwich-filled mouth wide open. With her bonnet shading her cruel eyes, she looked like a gift-wrapped cement mixer.

GIFT-WRAPPED CEMENT MIXER

THE PRESENT EVERYONE DREAMS OF!

Don started to cry and this made Miranda laugh louder.

Only then Miranda heard the pit-pat-pot-pet of badger paws running behind her. It was Bill, who had finally got up his courage and was rushing towards her. As soon as she heard Bill, Miranda tiptoed up to Don and patted his head – hard – as if she was being kind. Really, she was whispering, "If you don't stop crying, I will follow you home and tonight when you are sleeping I will shave off all your tail fur so in the morning your family will think you're a rat! Now run away and look as if you're happy."

Don did his best to smile and ran as fast as he could all the way home.

Then Miranda started to walk very gracefully and to laugh like a tinkling stream in an enchanted forest. She waved her dirty paw at Don and called, "Goodbye, dear small squirrel. My, how I love all of nature and everything. La-la-la." Then her walking turned into more of a jog, or perhaps a run.

All this made Bill so happy he would have sung, if he hadn't been so out of breath. He was darting along behind Miranda over the hot, slithery sand, his paws a blur. He could see her lovely

31

bonnet, her swaying skirts and her dainty paws, which were now skipping like crazy.

Just when Bill was wishing he could see his beloved's beautiful badgery face, Miranda twirled round and smiled the kind of bashful and charming smile that would cast a spell on anyone, even if they had just seen her trying to punch a seagull – and of course Bill hadn't.

Miranda's feet moved like lightning. Before Bill could yell, "Stop, stop, I am in love!" Miranda skipped off like an oiled weasel racing down a slide on its tummy, and she was soon heading into the woods and out of sight.

"Oh, nonononono NO!" howled Bill. He was really out of breath now and had a stitch. "I bet she's in a hurry because she has to tickle a rainbow, or stand in the sunset so that it looks even more fantastic. OOHH!"

And while none of his friends noticed, Bill raced away to find his perfect badger. 🐾

CLAUDE

SMALL BUT
EXTREMELY
BRAVE

SECTION SIX

In which we can wish that everyone will stay
safe, but our wish might not work. Maybe there is
something wrong with wishing just now. I didn't
get breakfast in bed even though I wished for it very
hard. At least our old friend Claude the spider is still
very brave and still wants to look after everyone he
knows. Then again, he is only a very tiny spider...

That evening, after all his exhausting worrying
Brian was tired enough to be dreaming as soon
as his head hit his straw pillow. Although he was
really very brave, he often forgot it. In his llama
barn, his friend Claude had promised that he

would be very fierce if any monsters arrived in the dark. He was only a tiny spider, but they both knew he would do his best. Brian snuggled into his bed, surrounded by his crash helmets and life jackets and knee pads and all the things he hoped would make his life safer.

BRIAN'S EMERGENCY SAFETY KIT

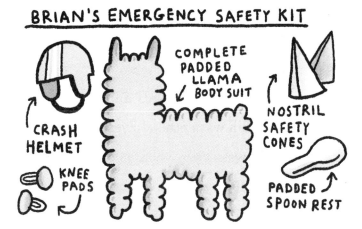

CRASH HELMET

KNEE PADS

COMPLETE PADDED LLAMA BODY SUIT

NOSTRIL SAFETY CONES

PADDED SPOON REST

As soon as Uncle Shawn was home, he sat in his big armchair and called, "Well now, Bill, it is time for us to have our cocoa and go outside and look at the sunset. What a very nice day we have had. I wonder what we will do tomorrow that will be even better?"

But nobody answered. And when Uncle Shawn went into the kitchen there was no sign of Bill. And when he saw the burned milk in the pan and the dirty spoons and the spilled cocoa he realised that the twins must have made their own bedtime drinks, because Bill would never have left so much mess – he was a neat and tidy badger.

Uncle Shawn tried calling, "Hello, hello! Bill, where are you?" He looked everywhere. He even searched in all the cupboards and looked up in the attic. But Bill wasn't there! Even though it was very late, Bill wasn't anywhere in the farmhouse!

"Oh, my goodness, where has he gone? I can't do without my best friend. What if he has got lost, or fallen and banged his knee and had to walk very slowly so that he isn't here yet?"

Uncle Shawn ran out to see if Bill was already in his rocking chair, waiting for the sunset. As he ran, he thought the farm seemed very big and empty and whistly without Bill. Over on the west side of the farmhouse were the two rocking chairs – a big human one and a little badger one. But Bill wasn't sitting in either of them!

Uncle Shawn didn't know what to do. "Oh dear. I wished that everything would be just right and my wish hasn't worked. That almost never happens. And where is Bill? Shall I wake up everybody and get torches and search the hedges? Shall I go to Pandrumdroochit and fetch Constable McNabb? Shall I call the fire station and get all the firefighters to search up high with their ladders and down low with their ropes?"

Meanwhile, down at Shoogeldy Bay something highly unexpected was taking place. If Uncle Shawn could see it he would be sure to wish that it wasn't happening.

But nobody's wishes seem to be working any more...

EGG → WITH EVIL INTENTIONS?

SECTION SEVEN

In which— oh goodness me, it's just too frightening for me to even describe any of it. I'll go away and have a mug of cocoa. Maybe hold a kitten, or a picture of a kitten, or a comfy blanket while you read this bit.

Down in Shoogeldy Bay innocent waves were patting the happy sand. The very big, bright moon was shining down peacefully. It was the third week of the full moon – which never usually happens.

But then – oh, dearie, dearie me – something began to appear out of the water.

Beyond the sunbathing rock (which was now a moonbathing rock) a pale shape was bobbing in the waves. It was round and looked like a great big egg. The egg seemed very determined and was moving quickly towards the rock.

When it arrived at the part of the rock where there were lots of footholds and handholds for people to climb, the egg rose up out of the water and – OH NO – it had a face!

It had staring, bulging eyes and a pointy nose and its mouth was strange and squishy. If you had taken one look at it, you would have screamed. Because it wasn't an egg at all – it was the big bald bitter head of a man! And, slowly and sneakily, the owner of that head oozed up onto the rock. If you had been brave enough to peek through your fingers at him, you would have seen his very white, skinny shins and his long yellow toenails and his strong, wiry arms that were the colour of unhealthy mushrooms. You would also have seen that he was wearing nothing except old, grey underpants and an old, grey vest.

And then you would have watched the man punch the air with his fists and jump up and down higher and faster than those famous and high-leaping acrobats, the Big Bavarian Bouncing Badgers.

But he wasn't jumping up and down because he was happy, or because he was trying to entertain a crowd of excited young badgers. No. The man was jumping because he was angrier than a thousand wasps who have been promised jam for dinner and have been served gravel instead. The

HOW ANGRY ARE YOU? A GUIDE FOR THE UNCERTAIN

① ARE YOU AS ANGRY AS A THOUSAND WASPS WHO HAVE BEEN SERVED GRAVEL INSTEAD OF JAM?

② AS FURIOUS AS 500 MICE WHO THOUGHT THE GREAT FESTIVAL OF SNEEZES WAS GOING TO BE THE GREAT FESTIVAL OF CHEESES?

③ AS BOTHERED AS A HOT BATTERED BADGER?

④ AS TETCHY AS A VERY IMPORTANT PYTHON WHO HAS CAUGHT THE WRONG TRAIN (AND NOW CAN'T SWALLOW IT)?

man was so furious he would have frightened a dinosaur – even a huge one with lots of beautiful scales and kind friends who made it feel confident about itself.

The man glowered and shook his fists so fast they were just a smear of rage in the moonlight. Then he yelled, in a cold, slidey, creepy, cruel voice, "I'WOO EGGOO UGGLESHAWN!"

The man had no teeth, so it was difficult to understand him as he yelled, crosser than crosswords.

The noise woke up some seahorses who had been dozing in the shelter of the rock. They listened and then – oh dear – they worked out what the man was saying.

And it was…

"I'LL GET YOU UNCLE SHAWN! I'LL GET YOU AND YOUR STUPID LLAMA FRIENDS! I'LL GET THAT FAT, SILLY BADGER AND THOSE TWO PECULIAR TWINS! I'LL RUIN

EVERYTHING YOU LOVE AND THEN I WILL GET YOU SO THAT YOU ARE MORE GOT THAN ANYONE HAS EVER BEEN GOT IN THE HISTORY OF GETTING!"

He had to stop for a minute after that, because he was out of breath. But then:

"I MILL HABEYE WEWENGE!"

You would have been terrified by the way he screamed this, even though it sounded like a very loud baby chewing a rubber toy.

What the man was trying to say was actually: "I WILL HAVE MY REVENGE!"

Then the man delicately brushed the tiny fragments of sand and seaweed from his feet (of which he was very proud), jumped off the rock and started to swim towards the shore, going quicker than the smell of bad sandwiches on a bus.

SECTION EIGHT

*In which— Oh, but where has Bill gone? I do
wish that he's safe and well, wherever he is.*

While horrifying things were happening at
Shoogeldy Bay, inside Brian's barn Claude the
spider had woven a big sign that said:

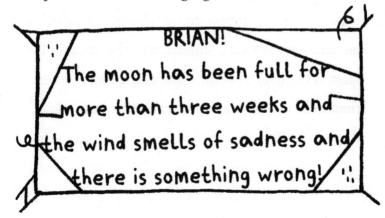

BRIAN!
The moon has been full for
more than three weeks and
the wind smells of sadness and
there is something wrong!

But, of course, Brian was asleep and couldn't read it.

So Claude tried shouting, "Brian! Brian! Something is wrong!" Spiders have very quiet voices because of being so small and Brian didn't hear. "Oh, I wish I was louder," said Claude, but his wish didn't work. So Claude rolled up the silk in his message to use again later and set off to find out more about what might be wrong. He wasn't walking to the moon, just to the farmhouse, but that's a very long way when you have teeny spider legs.

Inside the farmhouse Uncle Shawn had woken Sam and Sky and they were about to go to the llamas' barns to wake them up so they could all look for Bill. They could cover the distance more quickly than a spider because they had longer legs (especially Uncle Shawn).

As Uncle Shawn and the twins headed away from the farmhouse and Claude headed towards it, Guinevere and Carlos were in their llama barn. They were lolling in their hammocks, snoozling and snarzling. Uncle Shawn and the twins tiptoed inside the barn and then shouted a lot to try to rouse them. But they shouted quite quietly, because it seemed a shame to wake them when their long llama faces looked so happy. (They were both dreaming about biting each other.)

When Uncle Shawn and the twins reached the next barn, they found Ginalolobrigida had put a sign on her door which said:

ABSOLUTELY NO ONE ALLOWED IN. A LLAMA IS ENJOYING HER BEAUTY SLEEP AND MUST NOT BE DISTURBED UNLESS FOR A TERRIBLE EMERGENCIA.

"Goodness me," said Uncle Shawn. "I'm hoping this isn't a terrible emergencia..." He rubbed his wiggly hair to make himself feel better, but it was lying down very flat on the top of his head as if it were worried too. "I suppose I should just start yelling Emergencia as loudly as I can, the way the llamas do when they are having a Spanish emergency. That would wake everyone for sure."

But just then Uncle Shawn heard a wonderful soft thumping sound that was getting closer. It was just the nicest thumping he had heard all day:

UNCLE SHAWN'S BEST FRIENDS DANCE

START

THE SOFT SHOE SHUFFLE

BISCUITS!

SMILE
WINK
SMILE

WIGGLE KNEES AND GIGGLE

STICK YOUR TONGUE OUT LIKE A SQUIRREL

it was the unmistakable sound of Badger Bill's very own badger feet.

Uncle Shawn wriggled and jiggled and started doing the special dance he had invented called Best Friends. Then he spun round and put out his arms for a great big hug.

But then…

No hug.

No badger friend joining in with the dancing.

No, "Hello Uncle Shawn, I'm sorry that I came in late and made everyone wonder if I had been eaten by a lion, or kidnapped by pirates who forgot to leave a note."

Bill was just a badger-coloured streak of movement that pelted past Uncle Shawn, heading for the farmhouse.

"Bill," called Uncle Shawn to the speeding badger. "Where have you been?"

"Can't stop. I have important things to do," Bill's voice called back.

Uncle Shawn stood with his hands in his pockets and frowned. "Hmmm. Something has happened to my friend. I do hope it is a good thing, but I wonder..."

SECTION NINE

In which we learn about the dangers of
shopping online when you are in love.
Especially if you are a badger in love.

Upstairs in his bedroom, Bill was tired, too tired
to tell Uncle Shawn anything. And he was much
too in love to think about anybody apart from
HER. Her charming furry knees, the feminine
tilt of her ears...

Bill was covered in earth and bits of leaves,
and he was making his neat quilt with its pictures
of badger explorers very messy, but he didn't care.
He was IN LOVE. WITH HER.

The lady badger had run deep into the woods and Bill had tried to keep up, but somehow he hadn't quite managed. As it got darker and darker, branches had started to slap Bill on the nose and he tripped over tree roots and bruised his shapely badger knees. But he just couldn't find her.

In the end Bill had simply sat down on a tree stump and cried.

But just when he was despairing, he had heard a delicate and ladylike badger voice crooning, "Remember me... I know we will meet again..."

Lying on his bed, Bill could still hear those velvety tones. "Remember me, Badger Bill..." the voice had said.

If he hadn't been so exhausted he would have done his happy dance – spoof-spiff-splaff-spuff – and wiggled his tail in time to the beat.

If he hadn't been so much in love, he might have wondered how this peculiar badger covered in ruffles had managed to find out his name.

Bill began to imagine all the wonderful things he would do with this magnificent and kind new badger once they had met. Because of being in love they were bound to have much more fun than he did with the llamas, or the twins, or even Uncle Shawn. Bill felt a bit strange when he thought of spending less time with Uncle Shawn, listening to jokes and laughing and eating toasted cheese...

But surely the most perfect badger in the world would tell the most perfect jokes and make the best toasted cheese ever. Life was going to be fantastic and they would play and swim and hold hands and pick wildflowers.

Wildflowers! Of course!

Bill went to his little desk, turned on his Big Badger Supply Company computer and went online, even though he wasn't supposed to use his computer late at night because its glary light stopped him sleeping. But he wasn't going to sleep anyway – he was too in love!

He quickly spent all of his pocket money on a pink bow tie and a pink straw hat and a half pint bottle of Essence of Meadow Perfume. It said on the label:

Badgers courting and in love
Can give their romances a shove
With meadow smells and flowery pongs
Sweeter than chocs or soppy songs.

He was going to smell of wildflowers at all times. "I bet girl badgers would like that," Bill thought. "And it would help the finest girl badger in the world to like me."

Bill paid a little bit extra to the Big Badger

Supply Company for everything to arrive As Soon As Possible, because romance is all about being in a great big rush.

When he had finished ordering, Bill smiled. "I will be dashingly handsome in my bow tie. My straw hat will make me look like a cowboy, or an international badger superspy like Quentin Hudrock (licensed to stare), who finally discovered where socks go when they sneak out of washing machines at night. Everything I wear will be pink, because that must be her favourite colour. It might give me a bit of a headache, but I won't care. Oh, I do hope she likes me as much as I like her." He sighed a sigh so powerful that his windows rattled and he blew his poster of Quentin Hudrock in the film *Plimsolls Are Forever* right off the wall.

"I bet I'm more in love than any badger has ever been," Bill told himself, and his heart felt enormous and then tiny and then full of glitter.

"I wish, I wish, I wish that we will be happy ever after. This is going to be great." 🐾

DARK FOREST

SECTION TEN

In which we find out more about that terrible shouty person who climbed out of the sea. I hope he isn't a dreadful villain who is planning to do horrible things, or a criminal wanted in every country on Earth. And there are teeth!

And while everyone else was asleep, what was happening in amongst the trees of Shoogeldy Wood?

Are you sure you want to know? Really sure? Because I don't really want to have to describe it. It's something quite horrible.

It is a very important (and very terrifying) part of the story though, so everyone should know about it. But maybe you should read it while you hold someone's hand. As long as you can find someone who isn't busy making hats, or doing long sums, or combing a lion, or doing any of the other strange things that human beings do.

Miranda Badger, you will remember, was not at all as lovely as she pretended to be. She was the kind of badger who would put a hedgehog into a biscuit tin, as soon as she had kidnapped a hedgehog and eaten all the biscuits in the tin, shoving them into her mouth with both fists and letting dribble ooze down her chin. When she ran away from Bill and into the trees of Shoogeldy Wood, she knew that would make him want to speak to her even more than he already did. But she didn't go into the woods just to torment Bill. She was also meeting someone...

In a damp-smelling clearing Miranda called, "Hello? Hello?"

"Ow!" said a patch of darkness in a smiley

sneaky voice. "That was my foot! You know I have precious and beautiful feet. I could have had a career as a sock model! And you've trampled through the undergrowth like a brass band. This is supposed to be a secret meeting!"

"You're the one shouting!" snapped Miranda. And she turned on the torch she kept in the frilly pink pocket of her frilly pink nightmare dress.

In the torchlight she saw something that made even her tiny, gristly heart shudder. Hopping

round and round, holding one of his big, bare feet, was a pale, bald man wearing a pair of trousers that were much too short for him and a tiny flowery blouse.

Oh no! It was that angry, shouty man who climbed out of the sea earlier!

When the man stopped hopping and turned to face Miranda, she could see his raging eyes that seemed very keen to leave his head (as anything sensible would be), and his cruel nose that didn't enjoy smelling anything, and his growling lips that didn't enjoy saying anything – and teeth that suddenly popped straight out of his mouth so that he had to catch them quickly, fighting to get a grip on their slithery, slippery surfaces.

"Nggn! Eez eff!" He growled and shoved the teeth back in again, although they didn't fit him at all and seemed to belong to a much bigger person who might actually be a horse. "Nggn! These teeth. I found them in a bin and they're terrible!"

He had indeed found them in a bin at the back of the Pandrumdroochit Horse Hospital, which might explain a lot.

The man ground his big gnashers and then yelled, "And why is the postman so short? I had to steal his trousers and they don't fit at all!"

He had indeed slithered into the postman's garden and stolen his trousers off the line. Jemima the postman's cat had seen him, but she was a little bit too large and sleepy to do anything about it.

"I'm not sure if that blouse suits you. The pussy-bow is a bit out of date," sniggered Miranda.

"It was all I could find! There was nothing to steal on anybody's washing line. I had to wait until an old lady went swimming and steal her blouse from where she left it. Stop laughing. Otherwise I shall hypnotise you to think you're a nursery school teacher and you'll have to spend hours and hours every day being nice to tiny children and reading them stories."

The man grinned with his alarming teeth and it seemed that they might pop out at Miranda and bite her nose, or just slide down her face, leaving a big trail of furious saliva.

Miranda shuddered. She couldn't look at a small child without wanting to make it cry and tell it stories about people getting eaten by the wolves that live under their beds. (Which aren't true – there are no wolves under your bed. The Bed Goblins would eat them.)

THINGS MIRANDA SAYS ARE UNDER YOUR BED

① WOLVES

② MONSTERS ③ GHOSTS

THINGS THAT ARE ACTUALLY UNDER YOUR BED

① DUST ② CRUMBS

③ FRIENDLY BED GOBLINS

The man shouted, "This is all Uncle Shawn's fault. I used to have trousers that fitted and underpants that weren't full of sand. I was rich and powerful and I could make as many people unhappy as I wanted to and he spoiled everything!" He stamped his bare feet and immediately regretted it, because he trod on some nettles and they woke up and stung him. "Aggghh! Have you at least made that disgusting, fat badger fall in love with you?"

"Of course." Miranda fluttered her eyelashes and simpered. Seeing it was worse than toothache.

"I can't think why. You're the ugliest thing I've seen since I was inside that whale." He growled again. "And whose fault was it that the whale swallowed me? It was Uncle Shawn's fault!" Then he became very quiet and still and his eyes glittered. "I, Sylvester Pearlyclaws, will not rest until I have the biggest and nastiest revenge in the history of getting your own back." He licked

WANTED

SYLVESTER PEARLYCLAWS

ALSO KNOWN AS DR PEARLYCLAWS, CAPTAIN FOOST & OLD GRANNY MACHET

VERY GUILTY OF ALL THE CRIMES THERE ARE AND SOME WE CAN'T MENTION!

IF YOU SEE HIM – RUN AWAY! AND THEN CALL US AT ONCE AT 0800-HELP-OOH-WAAGH

(NEVER TAKE SWEETS FROM THIS MAN!)

STOP PRESS! Paris is reeling after international spoilsport and villain Sylvester Pearlyclaws released a magical cloud of vapour which dissolved all sports equipment, board games, yo-yos, dart boards and computer games. There is literally no fun anywhere! Asked for comment, Jean Claude, a small child, could only say, "Bof!" and cry while holding the string of his dissolved kite.

his huge teeth. "Now, let us discuss the next stages of my plan." And he led Miranda away to his secret den...

Oh no!

Sylvester Pearlyclaws is back!

Sylvester Pearlyclaws, the world's most terrible criminal, who is wanted in every country on Earth for doing terrible things (like covering Belgium in odd socks), is back!

Last time Pearlyclaws tried to be wicked, Uncle Shawn stopped him and asked a whale to swallow him up and not spit him out until he had thought about being kinder. But Mr Hubb the whale didn't really want a grumbling, nasty person in his tummy, so as soon as he guessed Pearlyclaws was safe to let go – BLEOOOOOG! Out came Pearlyclaws, surrounded by a big cloud of whale vomit.

And as soon as he was free, Pearlyclaws – who had won badges for swimming – headed as fast as he could towards Shoogeldy Bay and Uncle Shawn and WEWENGE!

No, not that. Wewenge sounds like a kind of unpleasant cheese and that's not very scary.

No, Pearlyclaws wanted ...

...

...

... REVENGE!

PANCAKES (on fire) →

SECTION ELEVEN

In which we find out more about falling in love. We also find out that you might not want your breakfast cooked by llamas.

The very next morning, Uncle Shawn walked into the kitchen and announced, "Bill, I think I will have toasted banana and egg sandwiches today."

But Bill wasn't there. Brian was sitting at the kitchen table and staring at a dish full of burning pancakes. "Emergencia," Brian whispered, because he didn't want to offend Carlos, who had been trying for hours to make not-on-fire pancakes.

Guinevere, who *did* want to offend Carlos,

was saying things like, "Congratulations. I did not think you could be any more stupid than you already are, but you have managed!"

"Oh, goodness," said Uncle Shawn. "I think Bill's cooking lessons haven't quite worked on us yet."

He quickly poured cream over Brian's pancakes, which put them out and made them a lot more delicious.

"Perhaps I should make us all porridge."

Uncle Shawn was trying to find the big porridge pot when he heard a pounding at the farmhouse door.

When he opened the door he saw the postman, who was very out of breath and holding an enormous parcel. "Oh, hello Uncle Shawn. I had to run all the way here because this had to be delivered As Soon As Possible," wheezed the postman. "I'm late because I could only find my second-best trousers this morning and they aren't quite loose enough for running."

Before Uncle Shawn could offer Postman Hamish a glass of lemonade, badger footsteps thundered down the stairs.

"My parcel!" said Bill. "Oh, hello, Uncle Shawn. I hope you made breakfast. I won't be able to any more, because I am in love with the loveliest badger in the universe so we'll be together all the time now..."

Bill opened the big parcel with his clever badger claws and put on his new pink hat and then took out his new pink bow tie and tied it round his neck in a lumpy kind of bow.

Uncle Shawn was a bit surprised by all this. "The loveliest badger in the universe? That sounds nice. I hope she is a kind and fun sort of badger, because you are a kind and fun sort of badger and

badgers who are in love might want to match."

"Yes, yes, yes..." muttered Bill, spraying his freshly delivered Essence of Meadow perfume all over his fur and not paying attention. He paused and sniffed. "Perhaps I need just a bit more perfume." And Bill started to spray all over again, waving the huge bottle about until every hair and bristle and whisker was dripping and letting off gusts of scent.

"Um, Bill?" coughed Uncle Shawn. "I do like the smell of meadow, but maybe that might be just a little – *Achoo!* – a little bit too much. My eyes are watering and my ears hurt. By the way, what is the name of this badger?"

"Um, well, I don't know her name yet," Bill replied. "But all badgers love meadows and I know she loves pink..."

Through tears caused by the perfume, Uncle Shawn looked at his friend and his strange pink bow tie and his unusual pink hat which was flattening his ears at a peculiar angle. "Well, Bill. I do hope this badger is fond of jokes and dancing and toasted cheese. We will be here if you need us. And maybe in the end our pancakes will not be even a tiny bit on fire."

But Bill wasn't listening. He left the box and all the bits of wrapping in a messy heap on the floor and simply scampered away in search of his beloved.

"Hmmm..." said Uncle Shawn, as the llamas popped their heads round the door to find out who had been upsetting a million daisies and squeezing a hedge, because that's what the hall smelled like now. "I hope this turns out for the best, but I am not sure that it will."

He went back to the kitchen and slowly made a big pot of porridge which tasted of being worried about a friend.

Meanwhile Ginalolobrigida Llama, who always woke up slowly, was still out in her barn, putting blusher and shader and shaper on her nose. (It was her best feature.) But the very tiny spot she'd had on her nose yesterday had grown bigger overnight. In fact, the more she stared at it, the bigger it seemed to get. And it was starting to turn a funny shade of red.

"I wish this terrible Nose Emergencia would go away," she thought. But the Nose Emergencia stayed exactly where it was.

"Oh, no! If a film director comes here looking for a magnificent llama to star in a romantic film they will not choose me because I look as if I am balancing an evil tomato on my face. I have a Face Emergencia!"

Ginalolobrigida sighed and tried dabbing powder on the spot. The powder only seemed to make it annoyed. 🐾

SECTION TWELVE

In which we find out what Pearlyclaws' signature looks like. This section may contain traces of Inverness. And there is also something extremely terrible in this section. You may wish to cover it with a cloth before you read on.

Meanwhile, Sylvester Pearlyclaws had hidden in a smelly bin lorry and was being driven right the way into the big city of Inverness. When he arrived, he slipped out of the lorry – smelling a little bit of rotten fish and mouldy vegetables – and marched into the city's biggest bank.

"Behold! I am Sylvester Pearlyclaws! I wish to open my deposit box."

The bank manager was surprised to see Pearlyclaws wearing a postman's trousers and a frilly blouse and ponging of thrown-away onions and kipper. But when he asked for Pearlyclaws to sign his name the signature was correct. (It said Sylvester T. Pearlyclaws and was followed by a frowny face.)

Sylvester T. Pearlyclaws 😠

And Pearlyclaws stared at the manager with his hypnotising eyes and convinced him that all was well, and perhaps the latest perfumes were all going to be based on kippers this year.

So Pearlyclaws was able to march into the bank's huge high vault and open his deep and long deposit box and pull out the deep and long drawer.

Inside was a big bundle of money and lots of stacks of paper with titles like:

EVIL BUSINESS PLAN 56
NOSE JEWELLERY

EVIL BUSINESS PLAN 28
DREAM CATCHERS

EVIL BUSINESS PLAN 12
EAR JEWELLERY

EVIL BUSINESS PLAN 57
SAWDUST ICE CREAM

The box also held a fake moustache, a doll in the shape of Uncle Shawn with lots of pins stuck in it, a small book with the title *Why I Hate Llamas: A Poem in 600 Verses* and – oh, no! – the biggest, heaviest, shiniest and sharpest pair of scissors you can imagine.

In fact, please don't imagine them. They're too scary.

Pearlyclaws lifted the scissors with his powerful wiry arms and waved them about, opening and closing the blades. They had been kept perfectly dry and oiled in the box. As he moved the handles, the blades glittered and made a terrifying sound…

SKROOSH, SCREEESH, SCHROOOOSH, SCHREEEEESH.

If you had heard them, all your fur would have turned white and your whiskers would have drooped. If you happened to have fur and whiskers.

Pearlyclaws laughed, which sounded just like somebody clearing a drain with an angry hen tied to a stick. Now he had everything he needed for REVENGE! 🐾

SECTION THIRTEEN

In which Bill gets a new nickname. And
Miranda lies a lot and is very sneaky.

Badger Bill pounded out of the farmhouse with
his plump but handsome badger's knees rising
and falling faster than Claude the spider pretending to be a yo-yo.

He wasn't exactly sure how he would find his
Perfect Badger, but before he could wish very
hard that she would just appear – in fact before
he was even halfway to Shoogeldy Bay – THERE
SHE WAS!

Miranda Badger was standing next to a (not

squeezed) hedge and appeared to be having a lovely chat with a rabbit. She was laughing prettily, showing her rather brown teeth and clapping her dirty paws. The ribbons on her purple bonnet were swaying romantically in the breeze and the frills and ruffles on her purple skirt were rippling delightfully.

Bill's heart did a headstand so quickly that he almost got hiccups. "Oooooh-wooo," he said, not knowing how to speak to this amazing creature.

HOW TO SPEAK TO YOUR BELOVED

"OOOOOH-WOOO" "GURGLE"

" UM... " "EEEEK!"

Miranda let the rabbit go – she had been standing on his tail. As he darted away, she muttered, "Watch it, Sniffles. No more spying on me or you'll discover how much I like bunny pie."

"Um, I beg your pardon?" said Bill, who hadn't quite heard her.

Miranda fluttered her lashes. Bill felt himself falling in love even more deeply – like a badger sinking into a lake of happy (but lying) custard.

"Oh, I said Bunnypie," Miranda said. "You don't mind if I call you Bunnypie, do you? I don't know your name. I noticed you on the beach yesterday but I was too shy to introduce myself. I'm Miranda Badger."

She was actually as shy as a busload of clowns. She shook Bill's paw with a grip that would have crumpled walnuts.

This made Bill squeak. "Eep. I mean, hello. I mean, can I call you Twinklebiscuits?"

"No, of course you can't, you idiot."

Bill's heart, by this time, was completely confused – it had been upside down, flat on the floor, in the air and knocked sideways. "Oh," he murmured.

"I haven't got all day, Bunnypie. Hurry up."

"My name's Bill."

"That's a horrible name. How stupid your parents must have been to give you it. Hurry up and ask me to be your girlfriend and then introduce me to your llama friends and everyone else at your farmhouse."

"How do you know I live in a farmhouse?"

"Doesn't everyone?"

"And how do you know I have friends who are llamas?"

"I just guessed – llamas are very popular this year. Don't ask me so many questions. They hurt my dainty lady brain." She dabbed at her forehead with one paw. "Why don't you introduce me to any humans you know? Maybe one who's an uncle?"

"I know an uncle!" squealed Bill. "I know Uncle Shawn and he's my best friend and we have so much fun and tell jokes to each other and…"

Just for a moment Bill remembered how much he liked Uncle Shawn and how sad he might be if he left the farmhouse and only spent time with Miranda…

But then Miranda squeezed his paw again (which hurt) and rubbed his ear (which made him feel like happy custard) and said, "Bunnypie, I'm so tired I may faint. First let's go to my den and I will make us some delicious cocoa."

And although she looked about as likely to faint as a camper van, Bill let her lead him away… 🐾

(VERY) FULL MOON →

SECTION FOURTEEN

In which we find the whole moon.

(So this section is very full.)

Uncle Shawn was sitting in his rocking chair outside, because the Essence of Meadow was still all over the farmhouse. Not for the first time, Uncle Shawn thought, "The moon is not meant to be full and bright all the time. It should only really look full for about three days. Hmmmm. And my wishes are not working. In fact, lots of people's wishes are not working. Not every wish comes true, but at least some of them always do. And the moon is the land of wishes... Something must be very, very wrong up there. I wish I knew what…"

Before he could realise that wishing probably wouldn't help right now, another wave of terrifying perfume oozed up over his chin. "I do hope Bill is safe with all his falling in love." He frowned and wibbled his hair with one hand. "Hmmm…"

Sam and Sky came out to join Uncle Shawn. They were both trying not to sneeze too much – because of the perfume – and not to cry too much – because of Sky's problem.

"I don't want to be invisible any more, Uncle Shawn," said Sky. She wasn't too invisible just at that moment, because she was wearing her dungarees and her favourite T-shirt with stripes. It looked as if some clothes were out playing with no one inside them. Away from the farm, this would have terrified people. Or made them try to catch her and put her in the laundry.

"Maybe we could paint you with something so that we could see you," said her brother.

"Like what? I don't want to be covered in paint for the rest of my life. It would itch."

"Well, then something like … like…" Sam couldn't think of anything that would work. "Jam! We could paint you with jam."

"That would be horrible," snorted Sky. "I'd end up covered in wasps."

"But people would definitely be able to see you." Sam grinned – he was just being silly to cheer his sister up. "And they'd hear you – the wasps would be buzzing while they ate the jam."

"And stinging me!" Sky pinched her brother with her invisible pinching fingers – they were one of the few things she liked about being invisible. "And I asked Ginalolobrigida how much it would cost to cover me in make up every morning, and it would be more than all my pocket money forever!"

Uncle Shawn sighed. "This week began very nicely with rhubarb pies and sunshine, but now

HOW TO BECOME NOT-INVISIBLE

1 PAINT YOURSELF WITH JAM

PROBLEM: WASPS

2 PAINT YOURSELF WITH PAINT

PROBLEM: ITCHES

3 GET SOMEONE TO DRAW AROUND YOU

PROBLEM: THEN YOU CAN'T MOVE

4 SHOUT

HERE I AM! RIGHT HERE!

PROBLEM: YOU WILL BE TERRIFYING

5 WEAR A HAT

PROBLEM: YOU WILL STILL BE TERRIFYING

you don't want to be invisible and you can't wish yourself out of it and the moon looks very poorly indeed and Bill has started smelling like a compost heap in June. And there's a funny feeling in the air that makes me think worse things are on the way. Hmmmm." Then he leaned back in his rocking chair and rubbed his wriggly hair again. "Sky, I thought you were enjoying yourself. You can stand invisibly beside important people making important speeches and blow raspberries and tickle them. You can fart next to naughty boys so that everyone blames them for the smell. You could get a job in a Haunted House and be all of the ghosts and make all of the scary noises."

Sky nodded. "I know. I once farted next to the nasty Lord Mayor every time he went outside for a week and in the end he resigned. But I miss being able to hug people without making them scream."

Uncle Shawn looked very hard at the empty space where Sky's face probably was. "Are you

pandrumdroochit Noos

20p

LORD MAYOR RESIGNS!

SHOCKING FART PROBLEM

Page 3 - MAYOR BLAMES DOG FOR DREADFUL INCIDENT

Page 5 - BIFFO THE DOG ISSUES FART STATEMENT:

"I was at home sleeping on the sofa. I'm not really allowed to, but everyone else was out so I thought I'd try it. If there was a fart at the town hall, it wasn't mine."

Biffo

really, really sure that you want to be just an ordinary kind of little girl, with only the usual wonderful things that are good about you?"

"Yes, I really, really am."

"Then we must go to the moon! As everyone knows, it is the land of wishes!"

The twins just had time to say, "But we don't know that!" before Uncle Shawn jumped up and clapped his hands. "How lumptious! I haven't been to the moon in ages! We need the giant soup dish. This will be such a simple adventure we won't even need a plan!"

Sam and Sky stared at him. They weren't quite sure if he was joking. But if anyone they knew had been to the moon, it was bound to be Uncle Shawn. 🐾

BIG METAL CHEST

KEEP OUT

SECTION FIFTEEN

In which we find Miranda Badger's home. That
means you should probably wash it at once
and then wash your hands and stand outside
for a bit. This section also contains a reminder
never to drink cocoa if it is badly spelled.

Miranda Badger's nasty, dirty den looked like a
cave that hadn't really bothered. In one corner
dozens of flouncy, brightly coloured frocks were
heaped up like a terrible accident in a flower
shop. In another corner there was a smoky little fire burning inside a ring of stones. With no
chimney the smoke just hung about miserably by

the ceiling, wanting to play outside. Near the fire was a biscuit tin and a carton of milk. Bill's sensitive badger nose could tell that the milk was sour without going anywhere near it.

There was one moth-eaten chair you wouldn't have been surprised to find in a rubbish dump. (Which is exactly where Miranda did find it.) The only other thing in the dusty den was an enormous metal chest.

"I have only just moved in and all my furniture and tapestries and the grand piano and the Ming vases are still in storage," Miranda said. She smiled like an open trap.

Bill tried to think of something polite to say like, "You have a home that is as lovely as you are." But that would have been like saying, "You smell of mouse droppings and make me want to take a shower." He decided to just stay quiet.

Miranda opened the big chest and rummaged inside.

"Can I help?" asked Bill.

"No you can't and don't ever look in this chest!" snapped Miranda, her wide bottom in the air as she clattered and clunked all the mysterious objects that were inside.

She stood up and waved a dented (and not very clean) saucepan in one paw and a tin marked "SPESHUL COCOA" in the other. She remembered to smile and cooed to Bill, "And now I will make you my special treat…"

She sloshed the sour milk into the pan, added brown powder from the tin, then stirred it all up like a maniac with a bit of stick. After that she

set the pan in the fire to heat up. Even though Bill was very fond of cocoa, he had never heard of SPESHUL COCOA and he knew that the milk would be lumpy and taste like angry ponds and earwigs, even if the cocoa was really Speshul. But he was too much in love to complain. He slipped out of his embarrassing pink hat and bow tie.

"Oh, thank goodness you got rid of those." Miranda laughed. "I hate pink now."

She handed Bill an old can filled with cocoa and he tried to swallow it down.

As he spluttered, Miranda rubbed his ears and whispered, "If you love me, you'll drink it all until the very last drop. That's a good Bunnypie."

"Aren't you going to – bealgh – have some of this – oooffff – lovely – yeuoogh – cocoa yourself, my dear?" Bill managed to ask, his eyes watering.

Miranda whacked the back of his head with her paw and made his thoughts rattle. "Silly badgers get love taps on the back of their ninny

noodles. I don't drink cocoa – it would be bad for my delicate and slender figure."

(Miranda was not especially delicate and slender. She was as solid as a post box and much the same shape.)

Bill tried not to say "Ow!" in case he upset his beloved's feelings, and finished the last of the cocoa – which was mainly the worst slimy curdled bits.

Miranda smiled and then, before Bill could ask her what her favourite type of pancake was, or if she liked watching films, or liked him—

POOMFF.

Bill fell into a deep, dark sleep, full of wiggling ghosts and jiggling toasts and giggling roasts, which rhymed but was very unpleasant.

I don't know about you, but I'm starting to dislike that Miranda Badger and I think there is something very bad in that SPESHUL COCOA...

SPACE
UNDERPANTS

SECTION SIXTEEN

In which there is planning for a real, live trip to the moon. Although I wish Uncle Shawn wouldn't leave now that Pearlyclaws is back. But Uncle Shawn doesn't know Pearlyclaws is back! Oh dear. Also in this section Bill gets called Silly Billy Bunnypie, which is very embarrassing.

Down at the bay, where the sky and the sea leaned against each other, the sun was setting in a big red line like jam and fire and golden things. Up above, the full moon was beginning to shine brightly, like the beautiful face of a Milky Moon Moth.

All the llamas were lined up on the darkening beach, waiting for Uncle Shawn and Sky and Sam to appear.

"I have not ever heard of anyone going to the moon without having a great big rocket and a spacesuit and space underpants and space boots," said Carlos.

"What if everything goes wrong and they can't get there and they just stay on the ground?" fretted Brian.

"Then they will still be on planet Earth where we live, you silly, silly llama," snapped Guinevere. "Why are they going to the nasty, far away old moon, anyway?"

"What if everything goes wrong and they DO get to the moon, but then they can't get back? And what will we do while they are away? And oooooooh…" Brian was now so worried he had run out of words.

Meanwhile, Ginalolobrigida Llama was thinking that none of this was as important as her nose spot, which was behaving very oddly and maybe turning into a boil. It was now almost big enough to be wearing its own hat. Before she could say this, two things happened at once.

Sam and Sky ran down to the beach wearing pullovers and thick trousers and woolly socks and hats because they had been told it was cold in outer space. Sky looked as if lots of winter clothes had decided to go on a trip to the seaside.

"Hooray!" all the llamas cried. "How brave you are! Or maybe very unwise! But hooray, anyway!"

From the opposite direction, a rather unsteady Badger Bill appeared, pulled along by Miranda (who was squishing his paw).

Bill's poor badger brain was woozy from the Speshul Cocoa, which had sent him to sleep for most of the day. But he had felt more and more cheerful as he got nearer and nearer to the farm and smelled all its familiar scents. He had missed everyone. Then his sensitive badger ears heard

everyone talking down at the bay and his sensitive badger nose smelled all his llama friends: Carlos, who smelled of peppermints and football boots and llama; Guinevere, who smelled of lavender and toffee and football boots and llama; Ginalolobrigida, who smelled of jasmine and roses and Lux Llama Powder Number 11; and Brian, who smelled of worry.

But the llamas were busy doing something exciting without him!

"Well done, Sam and Sky!" yelled Brian. "Although you will probably be lost in outer space!"

The llamas were too distracted by the thought of a moon trip to turn round and notice Bill. He somehow couldn't help thinking that they hadn't really cared when he went away. This wasn't right at all, but it made him decide that he'd show them!

"Llamas!" Bill bellowed. "This is my new girl-friend who cares about me – unlike all of you!"

Sky and Sam and the llamas turned round when they heard this.

Bill kept on shouting. "This is Miranda. She is my soulmate. A llama or a human could never be a true friend to a badger like me. Miranda can – she is a badger like me. Well, not like me – she's a girl, but you know what I mean." And he folded his arms and felt very peculiar and cocoa-ish.

"But Bill, we are for sure all your friends very much so," said Brian. "You are our *mejor amigo* best friend badger."

Miranda jabbed Bill in the ribs and sneered, "Oh, don't listen to him. What a feeble-looking llama – more like a tall goat. I bet his bandy legs are all covered in germs and about to collapse. And look at that boy – a very suspicious young human. I bet he licks other people's toffees and then puts them back in the wrappers so that nobody knows until they're sucking a slithery sweetie."

Sky gasped at this because it was so extremely rude and nasty about her brother.

BAD BEHAVIOUR : A GUIDE

BAD:

SECRET
INVISIBLE
FARTING

VERY BAD:

LICKING TOFFEES
AND PUTTING THEM
BACK IN THE WRAPPERS

THE WORST:

ABDUCTING
BRAVE YOUNG
BADGERS

"Oh and don't think I haven't noticed you, young Miss Farts-Everywhere-and-Runs." Miranda stared at the space where Sky's invisible eyes were. "You're going to be invisible and horrible for the rest of your life."

Although Bill was extremely in love, he felt sad as Sky's tears rained down like a sudden, tiny storm. "Miranda, dearest..." Bill began.

"Not now, Bunnypie. Boys who interrupt me end up with sore ears." Miranda clouted Bill's left ear so that it stung.

Bill tried to look brave, but inside his head half his ideas were going in one direction and the other half were crying in a corner – all except one terrific, shiny idea which was saying, "This is all sore and strange and sad, but Uncle Shawn could sort it out."

Just at that moment, there was a loud "WOO-HAY" and Uncle Shawn slid down the sand dunes, past Sky and Sam and the llamas, standing on what

looked like a big flat soup dish made out of metal.

"Here I am!" Uncle Shawn leaped off the dish as it surfed to a halt. "Hello, my best friend Bill." Uncle Shawn smiled at Bill with one of the friendliest smiles the world has ever seen.

But before Bill could let Uncle Shawn pick him up and swing him round so that his fur whiffled in the breeze, Miranda shouted, "Buncle Shawn! You're worse than that selfish bully Carlos, or that stupid bully Guinevere! Or that ugly Ginalolobrigida with her great big about-to-burst nose boil! You're even worse than that silly coward Brian!"

The llamas huddled together for comfort in the face of so many insults. Uncle Shawn stared in shock as Miranda finished by growling,

"You're the worst human being in the world. You don't care about anyone – only about having fun. Anything could happen to this badger and you wouldn't notice, not one bit!" She held out her paw to Bill. "Come on, Bunnypie. You can sleep on the nice damp dirt floor of my cave tonight."

Uncle Shawn was very sure that he didn't like this new badger one bit, and he didn't like the sound of anything she was saying. "But Bill," he said quietly, "we are going to go to the moon tonight. I would like you to come with us. You have always wanted to be a badger explorer and maybe see a Milky Moon Moth. The llamas have promised to look after the farm and not to set fire to the kitchen. Wouldn't you enjoy a moon trip?" Uncle Shawn gritted his teeth. "Perhaps your lady friend would like to come, too." (He really hoped that Miranda was allergic to moons and wouldn't come, because she would spoil anyone's fun.) "I bet you would be the first badger in space."

Bill's fur ruffled all over and his blood galloped in his veins. The moon! He could be the first badger on the moon and young badgers would grow up sleeping under coverlets with his picture on them – maybe one of him tickling the furry back of a Milky Moon Moth.

"Of course he doesn't want to do something so stupid and dangerous," interrupted Miranda.

All Bill's hopes stopped floating about happily and landed in his tummy with a bump.

But then Miranda softened her voice. "Oh, but Bunnypie. Shouldn't you stay in the farmhouse and keep an eye on those hideous— I mean, delightful llamas?"

Bill was completely confused by now. "I suppose... But the moon..."

"I'm sure it's nothing but dust and rocks. Why don't you take me back to the farmhouse and you can cook us a delicious dinner. I will count all of the valuables and ornaments and items of furniture inside … in case you lose anything. Silly Billy Bunnypie."

Bill felt himself blush as all his friends heard him being called Silly Billy Bunnypie. "I suppose we could do that… Couldn't I watch them go?"

"No. I'm hungry. Now let's get inside so that you can make me some tasty earthworm pie or fried nettles."

EARTHWORM PIE

And before he could say, "Have a nice moon trip, I wish I was going with you," Bill was yanked away, with another clout to his ear for no reason at all. As if there could ever be a reason for clouting anyone on the ear – especially a kind and wonderful badger like Bill. 🐾

UPSET LLAMAS

SECTION SEVENTEEN

In which there is important information about wishes

that all sensible people (and animals) should know.

Everyone on the beach watched Miranda's angry, flat feet pounding up the sand, her big bottom wiggling in her huge purple dress and Bill's little paws scrambling after her.

"Dear me," said Uncle Shawn. "If there wasn't something wrong with the moon and Sky didn't need to have her wish come true, I would stay here. But this will be a very simple trip with no problems or adventures. And I am sure nothing so terribly terrible will happen while we're away. At least, I hope so..." He wrinkled his forehead and wiggled his hair. "Then again, when people are in love sometimes they can seem very strange for a while before they get used to it. I wouldn't want to upset Bill if he is happy." Uncle Shawn shoved his hands into his pockets full of sand and toffees. "But how can any badger be happy with clouted ears? Hmmmm..."

Brian had recovered enough to say, "She was a horrible, horrible badger – very *antipático*. Her and her big, purple bottom are no good. Maybe sometimes we llamas fight and bite each other, but that is just for fun. We are never, ever as rude and cruel as she was."

The other llamas nodded and licked each other's ears and nuzzled noses for comfort.

"I hope she gets a boil on her face that swells until it is bigger than her head and that people come every day to point and laugh at her and take photographs," whispered Ginalolobrigida. This made her feel better, but only a tiny bit.

"My intelligent and wonderful and beautiful llama friends," said Uncle Shawn, "please keep an eye on Bill and try to be kind to each other, because I know that you do really like each other. And Brian – be as brave as you can be. I know that you are brave, because you are standing on a beach, even though you are scared of sand and water and the sky and seagulls."

"And seaweed." Brian nodded. "But I will be brave." And he smiled.

THINGS BRIAN IS SCARED OF
PART 79 : THE BEACH

THE SKY

SAND

SEAGULLS

SEAWEED

WATER

"Good." Uncle Shawn clapped his hands. "So now we must go to the moon."

"But why?" asked Sky. "I just want to stop being invisible. I don't want to be an astronaut. And we don't have any astronaut stuff. You're just playing a game to take my mind off being very sad, but that won't work because I'm not a little tiny girl any more!"

"Sky," said Uncle Shawn, "we are going to the moon because the moon is in charge of wishes. Once we get there, we can ask if you can have one so you can go back to being a non-invisible little – I beg your pardon – very huge and grown-up girl."

"But HOW?" asked the llamas, peering up at the moon along their four lovely llama noses and then peering back at Uncle Shawn as he stepped onto the big, round metal dish that clanged under his feet.

"How is the easy bit. The hard bit about going

to the moon is making your mind up to try." Uncle Shawn grinned. "Come and get into this iron dish Sky. Come on Sam. We will pretend we are soup in a gigantunormous soup dish." He giggled. "We'll be back almost before you notice we are gone," he said to the llamas.

"I already have noticed very much that you have gone," whispered Brian, but because he had promised to be brave he waved to Uncle Shawn and the twins and then he leaned a little bit against Ginalolobrigida for extra bravery.

Once Uncle Shawn and Sky and Sam were standing in the centre of the big iron dish – *clang, clang, clung, clung, clong, clong* – Uncle Shawn explained some more. "Everyone knows that the moon is the satellite of wishes – it catches all of the things people hope for during the night. Think of how many people look up and wish when they see the moon. That makes everyone who lives on the moon full of hopes and wish-helpfulness. If a

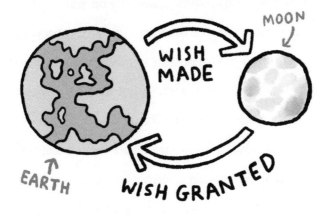

HOW WISHES WORK

WISH MADE

MOON ↙

EARTH ↑

WISH GRANTED

wish can come true, they make it happen as soon as they are able. All we have to do to make you into a visible person is hop up there and ask them for help. Then I'm sure your wish will be granted."

"Nobody lives on the moon," objected Sam. "And why are we standing in a big iron soup dish?"

"Because a nice French man with a magnificent nose told me an easy way to do moon travel. He was very clever."

Brian Llama shouted, "But the moon is so up there and you are so down here…"

Uncle Shawn smiled at Brian and winked a big, comforting wink. "Soon we will be on the moon sorting out whatever is wrong and then everyone's wishes will become possible again. And even little girls who don't want to be invisible any more can get their wish. Only, of course, Sky's face will be older when we see it – she won't be as little a girl as she was when anyone last saw her."

"But how will we get there and why is the moon in charge of wishes and how do you know about any of this?" asked the twins.

Uncle Shawn just winked another big wink and grinned a huge grin. He really did know all about getting to the moon. 🐾

CONFUSED ← BADGER

SECTION EIGHTEEN

In which we find Speshul Cocoa. So be
very careful not to drink any of it.

Up at the farmhouse, Badger Bill was sitting in
his rocking chair on the veranda, feeling very
confused and sipping more of the funny-tasting
Speshul Cocoa that Miranda had made for him.
(She had carried a packet of Speshul powder from
her cave in her handbag.)

Miranda was clumping about, counting the
forks and the pictures with shiny frames and
going through all of the cupboards and drawers
in the farmhouse. Bill wasn't very sure why.

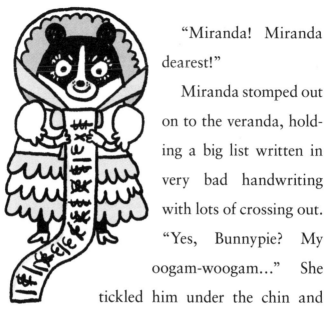

"Miranda! Miranda dearest!"

Miranda stomped out on to the veranda, holding a big list written in very bad handwriting with lots of crossing out. "Yes, Bunnypie? My oogam-woogam..." She tickled him under the chin and smiled a big yellow smile.

This almost made Bill faint with happiness, but he tried to concentrate. "Miranda, what are you doing in there? Why are you counting everything that belongs to Uncle Shawn and all of us?"

Miranda slapped him on the nose, which made him blink. "Silly bunny – I have to count your valuables in case they get lost or stolen and then sold for money while I'm in charge."

"In charge?" It seemed that she was in charge

of Bill's whole life now and maybe that was how love worked, but even so... "Why ... why would you be in charge, dearest one?"

Miranda poked him playfully under the chin (which really hurt). "Oh, but my stripey sweetheart, I have to be in charge. Buncle, I mean Uncle Shawn is going away to the moon and you're much too tired to do anything. Leave everything to me."

"But I'm always in charge when Uncle Shawn goes away." Saying this made Bill think again about how sad he was not to be going to the moon. "And the llamas know me and I make their lemonade just right."

Miranda giggled and the giggle sparkled in Bill's whiskers and made him feel sleepy. "Silly pinkie paws. I'll see to them."

"They're very special, sensitive, wonderful llamas..."

Miranda swatted his left ear – which was beginning to get really sore. "What nonsense,

Bunnypie. Now shut up and go to bed. I definitely won't have a secret meeting with anyone terrifying at midnight when you're all asleep."

"Mmm?" mumbled Bill, feeling his eyelids getting heavier. Miranda kissed his battered ear and this made him even drowsier, so he stumbled up to his badger bed.

RIGHT
EAR

LEFT
EAR

Far away at the back of Bill's head, something was nagging at him and making him feel uncomfortable. But he ignored it and snuggled under his quilt covered in pictures of explorers (none of whom had gone to the moon) and slid into a wavery, cocoa-ish sleep.

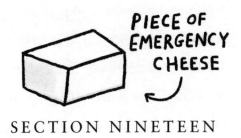

PIECE OF
EMERGENCY
CHEESE

SECTION NINETEEN

In which we go to the moon! Unless something

goes wrong! I hope nothing goes wrong!

Uncle Shawn and the twins were standing on the giant iron dish. Uncle Shawn was rummaging in the great big pockets of his great big coat. "I'm sure I have it here somewhere. Rhubarb sandwiches? No... Ball of string? No... Piece of emergency cheese? Ah, here it is."

He waved something about the size of a very big potato. It had a dull shine and the air around it seemed to shimmer the way it might on a very hot day. As Uncle Shawn moved the lump around, the iron dish shivered a little under their feet, as if it were a puppy that wanted to go for a run.

"This is the most powerful magnet in Scotland, maybe in the world." Uncle Shawn smiled. "Be sure to hold on tight when the soup dish starts to fly." He reached into his pockets again and brought out handfuls of rainbow-sparkling dust. "And keep hold of this – swallow it whenever you feel out of breath. It's powdered air."

"There's no such thing," said Sam.

Sky nodded, although nobody saw it.

"You'll see. Get ready…" said Uncle Shawn, reaching out both his long arms and waggling them about. "And hold on to your hats."

"We don't have any hats," complained Sky.

"And the moon is just the place to get them. Full of hats! Here we go!" And Uncle Shawn swung the lump in his hand back and forth. Everybody's hair – even the hair on their arms and their knees – started to wriggle about and stand up. The big metal dish shuddered underneath them.

"What's happening?" asked Sam, grabbing hold of Uncle Shawn's free hand.

Uncle Shawn laughed and held the magnet up as high as his chin. When he did this, the iron dish lifted itself clean off the ground and began to float in the air. "We're flying is what's happening," he said. He frowned a little bit. "I wish Bill could be here." Then he laughed again. "But it will still be wonderful – just you wait. And we can tell him all about it and maybe draw pictures of the most exciting bits."

Then Uncle Shawn held the magnet up over his head, as high as he could reach with his lanky long arms. This made the soup dish lift higher and higher off the sand.

"Oh, I don't know if I like this…" said Sam quietly, and he felt Sky hold his hand.

Sky giggled nervously. "Oh, Sam. Maybe, just maybe, I can be fixed." She hugged her brother and they both waited with their knees shaking a tiny bit.

Meanwhile, Uncle Shawn was looking very carefully at the moon. He tilted his head one way and then the other and then bent his knees a couple of times. The twins held their breath. And then Uncle Shawn swung his arms once, twice, three times and the dish bounced and biffed about until they felt quite queasy, before…

Uncle Shawn threw the magnet just as hard

as he could up into the hollow dark and towards the moon.

As you know, magnets attract iron. And, as you know, Uncle Shawn's magnet was the strongest in Scotland, so...

MOON TRAVEL: A GUIDE

1. STARTING POSITION
   MAGNET

2. THROW MAGNET

3. MAGNET ATTRACTS DISH

4. DISH RISES

"Ooooooaaaawough!" everyone yelled as the soup dish chased after the magnet, as fast as a dog chasing a stick. "Waaaagh!"

The twins kept on yelling as the dish rose up high enough for Uncle Shawn to catch the magnet. The soup dish slowed right down again and Sam and Sky were worried that they would start falling, but then— "Ohnooooaaaah!" the twins screamed as Uncle Shawn threw the magnet again and the soup dish skooshed after it even faster than it had the first time and started to spin and spin.

As you may have worked out, all the stories about flying saucers in Scotland started because of Uncle Shawn and his giant iron soup dish darting and spinning and bouncing about on his trips to the moon.

"Wheee!" Uncle Shawn laughed. "Two friends and an excuse to go all the way up to the moon! Woo-hoo!" And he caught and threw and caught and threw the magnet, faster and faster.

The stars whirled and wibbled around them and the soup dish started to sing gently because it was going so swiftly. Under their feet, the lights – of all the houses and towns and streets and trains and squirrels reading with torches under the leaves – spread out and made patterns. In the end the whole of Scotland was gleaming below them, and then many other places beyond that.

Sam and Sky did think this was very exciting, but all of the stopping and starting and spinning was also making both the twins feel sick.

Then they both *were* sick: "Bleaugh! Bleooogg! Hooowah! Hhhhwooofff!"

Uncle Shawn had to be very quick to pick up Sky and hold her over the side of the soup dish. Then he put her down and caught the magnet and threw it towards the moon, then he picked up Sam and held him over the edge of the dish, then put him down and caught the magnet and picked up Sky again and… He was really busy for a while, making sure that none of the sick ended up in the soup dish. After all, it would be no fun whizzing about in a spinning soup dish full of vomit, even if you were getting an unexpected trip to the moon.

And *WOO* and *FFOO*, on went the big metal dish, spinning and spinning. 🐾

BILL ASLEEP

SECTION TWENTY

In which Bill is still sleeping a nasty Speshul kind
of sleep and there are some very unhappy llamas.

The following morning in the farmhouse kitchen,
Miranda was trying to be nice to the llamas. She
was wearing a luminous orange gown covered
in miniature orange cauliflowers and a pointy
orange bonnet. She looked like a road cone on its
way to a birthday party.

"Good morning, my friends," she chirped, smiling like an advert for evil dentures. "Good heavens!
That's grown!" She pointed at Ginalolobrigida's
spot with a flouncy orange parasol.

Ginalolobrigida glowered at her and the other llamas did some of their best angry staring.

Miranda just grinned back at them and whistled by sticking two fingers in her mouth and blowing very hard. This was unladylike and really loud.

As if he had been waiting just outside for the *PHWOO-EEEP* sound, in walked a stranger carrying a leather bag and a big case that could have held an extra-large banjo. He was wearing a very neat pinstriped suit and shiny, shiny shoes that stung your eyes if you looked at them. His shirt was brilliantly white and his long, large moustache flopped over what seemed to be very big teeth. And on his head he wore a massive red hat covered in rainbow feathers and tiny mirrors and buttons. It was the most distracting hat you could imagine.

It was a hat that could even distract four llamas who knew what Sylvester Pearlyclaws looked like.

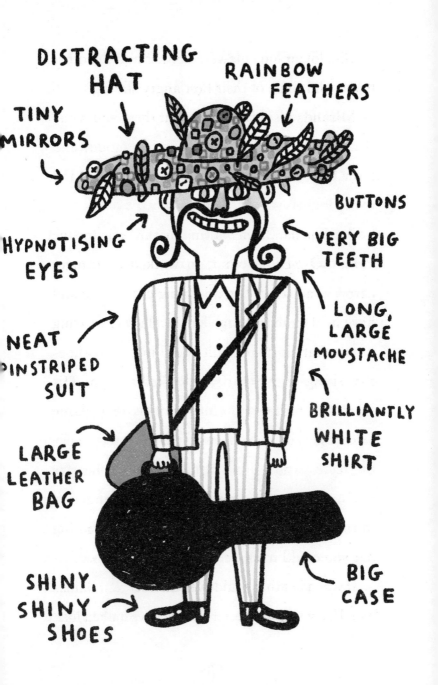

BUT IT WAS SYLVESTER PEARLYCLAWS AND INSIDE THAT BANJO CASE WERE HIS TERRIBLE SCISSORS!

OH NOOO!

"Hello," he purred in his sneakiest voice. "How wonderful to meet such resourceful llamas. It's such a shame that Uncle Shawn has run away and left you because he doesn't care about you any more." And he stared at the llamas with his hypnotising eyes so that they would begin to feel everything he told them was true.

"No, that is not true," said Brian. "He cares."

"Well where is he, then?" asked Pearlyclaws. Before anyone could answer he continued, "But have no fear – I, Sidney Smith, am here to help you. I am an expert in llama health and happiness." He stopped as he caught sight of Ginalolobrigida's nose. "Ah," he said, and his big teeth showed in a strange, ginger-whiskery grin.

"I am sure it is getting smaller," lied

Ginalolobrigida. "But I am not quite feeling myself."

Ginalolobrigida had always known that she looked as beautiful as she felt, but today, being examined by this strange Sidney, she was shy and a bit worried.

BUSINESS CARDS (completely fake)

Pearlyclaws slid up to her on his smooth and shiny shoes, set down his banjo case (which didn't hold a banjo) and reached into his pocket, bringing out a pot of green ointment. "Behold! Llama nose improver. Dab this on the affected area first thing in the morning and last thing at night and you will find your nose begins to sparkle like a jewel."

INGREDIENTS:

A MYSTERY. JUST DAB IT ON AND THE BOILS BE GONE! WORKS ON SPOTS, BOILS, PIMPLES (WILL NOT REMOVE DIMPLES) ALSO RESTORES SHINE TO SHOES, CLEANS OVENS and UNBLOCKS DRAINS!

Ginalolobrigida took the little pot and – even though it smelled a bit like ponds and bottoms – she decided to give it a try. "I wonder if he is the handsome stranger predicted by my horoscope," she thought to herself. "He mentioned jewels…"

"Well, llamas." Pearlyclaws stroked his moustache – although really he was making sure it was still stuck to his top lip with Mucho Macho Moustache Glue. "Let's get you outside into your barns. And do be careful, my dear, kind, intelligent llama friends." And Pearlyclaws giggled as if he was full of a terrible secret. "I don't want you to bang your noses…"

"Please, Señor Smith, may you perhaps play us a tune on your banjo so that we can go to sleep tonight? We are very worried and I think maybe we might have nightmares," said Brian.

Pearlyclaws laughed a laugh that sounded like trolls in a basement hitting each other with fish. "Dear, dear, cowardly Brian. I don't have a banjo in my case, but one day very soon – I promise you – I will show you the instrument I do have in there and then you will be able to sing as loud as you can."

As Pearlyclaws' eyes glimmered strangely and his moustache waved at them as if it wasn't their friend, Brian and the other llamas scampered away to their barns as fast as they could. They were beginning to find the odd man who was calling himself Mr Smith a bit too scary.

Oh, what will happen next? I don't think I can bear to guess. 🐾

BILL (STILL ASLEEP)

SECTION TWENTY-ONE

*In which there is a spider. But a nice spider. And
he is about to discover some horrifying news.*

At the farmhouse, Miranda was ticking items
off a very long list. "Piano, sink, forty spoons,
eight knives and sixteen jars of jam. We've taken
almost everything."

For hours and hours after the llamas had left,
Miranda and Pearlyclaws had been sneaking all
the nice things out of the farmhouse using the
back door – when they weren't searching for
secret treasure, just in case there was any. Most
of the rooms were looking very empty and some

had holes where Miranda had prised up the floor-boards, hunting for a chest of money, or maybe silver coins. (Even though Uncle Shawn didn't have anything like that.)

Pearlyclaws tugged off his moustache with a small scream – "*YeeE!*" – and snapped at her, "I don't care about jam and spoons, what about money? Uncle Shawn must have money. He's so generous to everyone and always giving presents and letting things stay at his farm for free – he must be rich!"

BILL ASLEEP

SYLVESTER AND MIRANDA PLOTTING

"We've searched everywhere, Sylv. We can check again – the Speshul Cocoa is keeping the silly, fat badger sound asleep and the llamas are busy being stupid outside. I won't let them back in. I'll say that the fresh air is good for them and they make too much of a mess in the kitchen – which they do, the hairy beasts."

As we know, Miranda was as messy as a football pitch after three weeks of rain, sixteen matches and a horse race, so she had a cheek saying that anyone else was messy.

THE BARN

WORRIED LLAMAS

"It's Mr Pearlyclaws to you." Pearlyclaws chuckled like a swamp clogged with wickedness and walked over to his extra-large banjo case. "And even if we can't find the treasure, we have the rest of our plan..." He flipped back the lid and – *Aaaah!* – revealed the giant pair of scissors!

When she saw them Miranda clapped her dirty paws together and shouted, "Oh yes! Llama nose jewellery! It's the latest thing. All you need is a few llama noses. And all you need to get llama noses is a big pair of scissors to snip them off!" She grinned with all her yellow, cruel teeth.

"Then we varnish them and stuff jewels in the nose holes." Pearlyclaws lifted out the scissors and opened and shut the two mighty blades so that he could see them shine and hear them make hungry noises...

SKROOSH, SCREEESH, SCHROOOOSH, SCHREEEEESH.

So Ginalolobrigida's horoscope had been

LLAMA NOSE JEWELLERY

IT'S THE LATEST THING!

A handsome and delicate brooch →

Hat ornament

Pretty earrings (FOR THE LARGER EAR)

Pretty finger rings (FOR THE LARGER FINGER)

Jewelled shoe buckles →

Coat buttons

right, but not in a lucky and enjoyable way at all. Pearlyclaws thought llama noses were like jewels, and he'd snip them off and make them valuable.

Those two wicked people were so pleased with themselves and their horrible plans that they jumped up and did a dance of wickedness.

But who was watching from a corner of the kitchen ceiling? Claude the spider. Spider super-spy Claude. He had walked all the way from Brian's barn. And now – he had to tell Brian what he had found out!

He set off again on his tiny legs, as fast as he could go. 🐾

SECTION TWENTY-TWO

In which there is an unexpected
kind of moon welcome.

While so many mainly terrible things had been happening on the farm, Uncle Shawn and Sam and Sky had been whooshing up through space towards the moon. Now they had stopped flying upwards and could feel themselves rushing faster than an oiled eel, down towards the surface of the moon! The magnet was falling even faster than they were and pulling the iron dish after it – more and more quickly, down they went. To the twins it seemed as if they would all land in one big squish and never be seen again. Or at least end up much shorter, like tin cans that someone has stepped on.

Uncle Shawn shouted to Sam and Sky, just as if he was having fun and not worried one bit, "Hold on to my ankles, please! I have to catch that magnet before it gets too quick!"

Sam and Sky had to really hold on tight while Uncle Shawn wriggled over the edge of the dish until most of him was hanging in outer space. As the twins held him and gritted their teeth, Uncle Shawn reached down and just managed to catch the magnet. It was going faster than an oiled penguin sliding down an iceberg because it is very late for dinner.

"Pull me in, please!" The children pulled Uncle Shawn back onto the metal dish and, as he stood up, the magnet's attraction slowed the dish a tiny bit.

But it still seemed they were going too fast to

survive a landing. The moon dust was billowing around them and Sky shouted, "We're going to end up like bicuits!"

"Like biscuits?" yelled Uncle Shawn. "Yes, I love them!"

"No, she means we're all going to end up like broken biscuits!" shouted Sam.

Uncle Shawn just winked and smiled and said, "Now please, if you can just help me get as high as I can..." And he jumped, holding the magnet over his head, and because he weighed almost nothing the twins were able to hold on to his knees and keep him from landing back on the dish.

Trying to get close to the magnet, the big iron

dish began to really slow down. In fact, it slowed down so suddenly that Sam and Sky felt their tummies go flip-flop as if they had just gone over a bridge.

Finally, with moon dust shining and powdered air glittering all around them, their peculiar spacecraft landed – FOOMFF – in a deep cushion of extra dust. They were safe!

"Brilliant! Well done! I couldn't have done it without you!" Uncle Shawn jumped up and down with delight and this made the soup dish jump up and down, too.

"Woo! Nooo! That's too bouncy!" shouted Sky.

Uncle Shawn laughed and gave each of the twins a big packet of powdered air to swallow as they went along, and munched down a big handful himself. After that they cheered and hugged, because they were so glad they hadn't been squashed.

And they were on the moon! They were really, truly on the moon! Hooray!

They would have kept on celebrating for some time – because moon dancing is great, bouncy low-gravity fun – if they hadn't been interrupted by lots of shadows. Some of the shadows were velvety dark grey, some were midnighty blueish and some were misty tumbles – and they had arms and legs!

If this wasn't worrying enough, one rather round shadow crept up and swallowed Uncle Shawn's wonderful magnet – GLUMP!

"Uncle Shawn!" called Sam. "Something has happened to your magnet! How will we get home?" Sam blinked and stared and – suddenly – he realised that shadowy creatures were blinking and staring right back at him. "And who are they?!"

"Everything is fine. These are some of the moon people, there's nothing—" But before Uncle Shawn could say "to worry about", the moon people closed in and picked up the big iron dish and carried them away!

At least, the moon people thought they carried all of their visitors away. But as you know, Sky is an invisible girl and it is very difficult to catch an invisible girl if she doesn't want to be caught.

Meanwhile, down on Earth another day was dawning – perhaps the most dangerous day that any of our friends had ever faced. 🐾

SECTION TWENTY-THREE

In which we find some good nose news
that anyone can see and some good
moon news that no one can see.

While so many terrible and strange and exciting things were happening to so many of our wonderful friends, Ginalolobrigida was delighted.

She had woken feeling better than she had in ages, and when she looked in her Llama Looking Glass she saw that her nose spot had almost completely disappeared. Mr Smith's mysterious ointment was amazing! She examined her face: the luscious llama lashes, the glowing and marvellous eyes, the glossy nose fur and the perfect tufts of hair on her delightful ears. "I am almost as beautiful as I feel inside." She sighed. "That Mr Smith is a magnificent friend to llamas everywhere."

Although Ginalolobrigida was very clever for a llama and right about lots of things, she was very wrong about that. "I look forward to seeing Señor Smith again." She smiled contentedly.

It was not the most sensible smile she had ever smiled.

Meanwhile, Brian Llama was turning over in his llama hammock and dreaming very alarming dreams about that new human Mr Smith chasing him with a big banjo that he was whirling about his head.

His hooves twitched while he dreamed of running and his head decided not to trust that Mr Smith, not even a little bit.

And meanwhile, back on the moon, Sky was smiling a very sensible smile indeed while her head whirred with lots of ideas.

She had been very clever and had wriggled out of her moon-going clothes and left them safely in the iron dish as the moon people rushed in to capture everyone.

This allowed her to be invisible and slip away without anyone noticing anything, except maybe getting their foot stepped on or a nudge in the ribs. And in all the confusion of the capture, no one really paid any attention to that except Uncle Shawn, who smiled a wise smile straight at a patch of empty air, which maybe wasn't empty at all.

After the moon people left with Sam and Uncle Shawn and the iron dish, Sky was left standing alone in the moon dust.

"Humph!" she said. "Well, I suppose being invisible is going to be useful for one last time. I shall have to rescue Uncle Shawn and Sam. Oh, but what will we do about getting home again? One of those terrible creatures swallowed the special magnet..." She felt so sad and alone that she sat in the dust and nearly cried. But then she decided that she really had to be brave, because everyone – Sam and Uncle Shawn and everyone in the world with a wish – was relying on her. "No. I will be brave and amazing and think of a fantastic plan!"

While Sky was missing her brother and the wonderful Uncle Shawn, and trying to think how she could save them all by herself, behind her two very bright creatures whose arms and legs were made of light and whose middles were made of sparks and glimmers came up and started playing in the dust, as if it were sand at the seaside. They

chased each other and caught each other and somersaulted down a big slope of dust and made dust castles. The faster they ran, the brighter they shone, with streams and fountains of lights flowing off them. Their movements made a very small noise that was quite jingly.

The jingling got louder as the young, shiny moon people dared each other to get closer and closer to a long line in the dust. Then a much bigger light creature ran up and shouted at the two little ones.

"Bad children! Don't ever play here again! This is much too near to where the Hurrfoofurrhurrs are. Now that we're at war with them, we can't risk it. Keep away from the border line!"

"But we like them," said one of the young light creatures.

"Yes, they're tickly," said the other. "Why can't we play with them any more? They like us, because we're warm and we jingle."

"No, they don't like you," said the older creature. "They're horrible. They've always been horrible. And we Paafoofurrhurrs won't be speaking to them or playing with them any more. We are working out how to be at war with them – maybe by never sending them birthday cards again."

"So the tickly midnight moonfolk are called Hurrfoofurrhurrs and the sparkly moonfolk are called Paafoofurrhurrs," thought Sky. "And even if they don't really know how to be at war yet, what if they find out and hurt each other?

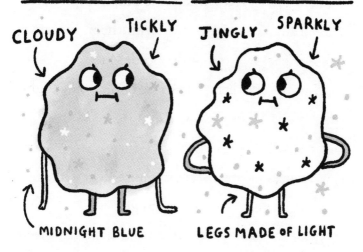

HURRFOOFURRHURR

CLOUDY · TICKLY · MIDNIGHT BLUE

PAAFOOFURRHURR

JINGLY · SPARKLY · LEGS MADE OF LIGHT

And what if they think Sam and Uncle Shawn are spies?"

As the big Paafoofurrhurr pulled the little ones away, Sky crept away to find where Sam and Uncle Shawn had been taken. Off she went, treading silently on the soft moon dust. She was very brave. 🐾

BILL (STILL FAST ASLEEP)

SECTION TWENTY-FOUR

In which there is sneakiness and pretending.

Back on the farm, Bill still hadn't woken up. Two nights and a day had passed since he staggered up to bed and fell asleep. He was trapped in his horrible Speshul sleep, full of nasty dreams where all of his teachers chased him and his tail turned pink and started to whizz round and make noises like a kazoo (which would embarrass any smart young badger). Around him the farmhouse was empty and full of miserable echoes and sad dust. During the night Miranda had even stolen some of the windows.

While Brian dozed in his llama barn – because his nightmares had made him extra-tired – the other llamas were all gathered around Pearlyclaws. He had told them they were having breakfast outdoors because it would be refreshing. Not because the kitchen had been stolen and if they went inside they would all notice.

Pearlyclaws – who was pretending to be called Mr Smith – was also pretending to love llamas. He even gave Ginalolobrigida, Carlos and Guinevere

SAD AND EMPTY FARMHOUSE

MISSING ROOF TILES

DUST

MISSING WINDOW

MISSING DOOR

scones that he said he had baked himself. (Really he had bought them from Mrs MacMuckle's World of Scones in Pandrumdroochit.)

Ginalolobrigida was especially nice to Pearlyclaws as she was so pleased that her nose was almost back to normal. She even lowered her head so that he could tickle between her ears if he wanted to. She was sure he was the marvellous stranger her horoscope had mentioned.

Of course, Pearlyclaws would rather have jumped into a tub of boiling scorpions than have to be nice to a llama, but he needed them for his terrible plan. He produced his measuring tape and started to measure how wide the lovely, soft downy ends of the llamas' noses were, and how long their ears were. Then he measured the size of their nostrils.

This made Carlos sneeze. "No one has ever measured our noses before, Mr Smith. Nor our ears."

"Who?" asked Pearlyclaws. "Oh, yes. Me. Mr Smith. I am Mr Smith." Pearlyclaws dabbed ointment on to each of their noses. It made their skin feel very smooth and their tiny nose hairs very glossy, but they thought this was all a bit strange.

"Mr Smith, do you have any horse relatives? You have wonderful horse teeth," said Guinevere.

"What!" yelled Pearlyclaws.

The llamas suddenly felt scared. If Pearlyclaws wasn't careful they might lay their ears flat along the sides of their necks and tip up their chins, and the next thing he would see would be a waterfall of llama spit heading his way.

"I beg your pardon," Pearlyclaws smarmed. "My mother was always being asked if she was a horse and teeth are a sensitive subject."

This was another huge fib. The only thing anyone ever asked his mother was, "Why are you so horrible and – goodness – why is your little son even worse?"

WINNER OF ULLAPOOL SCARIEST BABY COMPETITION (THREE YEARS RUNNING)

VOTED MOST LIKELY TO BECOME A MASTER CRIMINAL

MOTHER VOTED MOST LIKELY TO STEAL YOUR SHOES

Pearlyclaws put the ointment pot away and began to stare at each of the llamas in a hypnotising way.

"You are feeling sleepy. I am a qualified llama expert and you can trust me," he lied. "Hang on, aren't there four of you dreadful creatures? I mean, marvellous beasts."

"There are four of us... Hmmm... Yes, four," murmured Ginalolobrigida as she slowly sank to the grass.

"Four..." mumbled Carlos as he also sank down and started snoring.

"Hmmmm," muttered Guinevere as she folded up like a towel and fell fast asleep.

The three llamas were at Pearlyclaws' mercy! Oh no!

Pearlyclaws studied them. "This nose will be perfect for a brooch. And those ears can be added to a hat." He giggled. "And these ears are so dreadful I might just cut them off and throw them away. But first I am going to find that stupid, scaredy, knobbly-kneed llama with the sad eyes."

And then he laughed and skipped happily away to find poor Brian. "I'll get you, Brooin… Brown? Brain?"

Pearlyclaws couldn't even get Brian's name right.

If you would like to boo at this point, it might make Pearlyclaws feel a little less sure of himself.

Yes. There. He stubbed his toe on a clump of grass and hurt one of his precious feet that make him so proud.

Oh, but that hasn't stopped him being completely horrible. It has just made him annoyed.

"Yes," he growled, "there's nothing nicer than making an animal with sad eyes get sadder."

And he stamped onwards, determined. But with a sore toe.

• • •

While Pearlyclaws went sneaking and snooking along to find poor Brian, Uncle Shawn and Sam had been carried straight into horrible danger.

They were set down inside a large, warm cave, where the shadowy moonfolk surrounded them like a tickly fog bank.

Uncle Shawn helped Sam to stand. "I'm sure this will all turn out very well and that we will be having great fun in no time," he whispered, and he held Sam's hand.

LARGE
WARM
CAVE

But then a huge voice roared, "WHO HAS DARED TO ENTER THE TERRITORY OF THE GREAT AND GLORIOUS KING OF THE HURRFOOFURRHURRS? YOU ARE SPIES FROM OUR SWORN ENEMIES THE PAAFOOFURRHURRS! WE MUST PUNISH YOU!"

All the Hurrfoofurrhurrs backed away, and Sam and Uncle Shawn could see a giant, frowning creature, made out of swirls of shadow and gloom... 🐾

SECTION TWENTY-FIVE

In which we find a spiderweb, but not the clingy, scary kind – the really, really useful kind. There are also tippy-tappy spider feet.

Since hearing so many terrible and important things in the farmhouse, Claude the spider had been rushing – as fast as he could on tiny feet – back to Brian's barn. It had taken him all night climbing over blades of grass and walking round daisies and swinging through bushes like a tiny Tarzan.

He was hoping to save Brian. He was hoping to save everyone – if only he could get to the barn in time.

This morning, he was nearly there...

And who else do we know was heading for Brian's barn on this exact same morning – on big human legs and quick human feet, of which he was far too proud?

Pearlyclaws!

And he had stopped to collect those huge, sharp, nose-nipping scissors!

Claude the spider bounced up and down on Brian's nose with his pointy tippy-tappy spider feet.

"No, Señor Spider," mumbled Brian. "I am sleeping please and thank you. I am most extremely very tired and do not want new nightmares with spider feet inside them." And the hair on Brian's ears stood up a little bit because spiders made him nervous, even though he knew that Claude was really nice and helpful.

Brian rolled over. But then he felt another prickly dance of spider feet.

"Señor Spider Mr Claude sir. Please do not disturb me. I do not want to dream of spiders serving ice cream made with flies..." Although, of course, that's exactly what he started to dream about – very stern-looking spiders, waving tubs of bluebottle ice cream and shouting at him.

ICE CREAM FOR SPIDERS

Bluebottle Dream

VANILLA with Fly Clusters

HORSEFLY DELIGHT

mosquito Swirl

Claude jumped up and down even faster and waved six of his legs in the air while he bounced.

Brian rolled over to try sleeping on his back with his hooves in the air. This was very uncomfortable and he was just about to say, "Oh, Señor Claude, stop please," when he opened his eyes and saw Claude's enormous message all over the rafters and beams of the barn's ceiling.

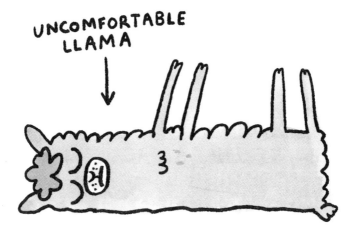

UNCOMFORTABLE LLAMA

Every single one of Brian's hairs stood on end so that he looked like a frightened fur balloon.

This was because the message said:

BRIAN! THAT TERRIBLE MIRANDA BADGER AND THAT AWFUL HUMAN BEING SYLVESTER PEARLYCLAWS WANT TO CUT OFF YOUR LLAMA NOSES AND YOUR EARS AS WELL! THEY WILL MAKE THEM INTO SAD JEWELLERY FOR CRUEL PEOPLE! AND THEY ARE GIVING BILL SLEEPY COCOA WHILE THEY STEAL EVERYTHING! DEARIE ME!

Brian froze in total panic. He couldn't imagine what he should do...

While Brian was being more worried than he had ever been before – which international worry experts would have thought was impossible – Pearlyclaws was on his way.

INTERNATIONAL WORRY EXPERTS

And he had almost reached Brian's barn!

As Pearlyclaws stamped angrily along on his beautiful (or so he thought) feet, his big horse teeth glimmered in the sunshine and so did the nose-snipping scissors he was carrying. And he was smiling!

Brian's llama barn had a big BRIAN painted on its door with a smiling llama face saying "Hola amigo!", which means "Hello friend!". (Brian had spent a whole afternoon with a can of orange paint, writing it all by himself.)

But maybe there was still a chance Pearlyclaws wouldn't remember that Brian was called ... well, Brian. Then he would go and look in the other, empty barns and maybe get fed up and go away. Or need to sit down and have a rest, or—

Oh, but no! Pearlyclaws had finally remembered that Brian was called ... well, Brian. This made it easy for that very wicked man to find where that lovely llama was defenceless and sleeping...

Pearlyclaws snickered as he opened the big barn door.

He stepped inside, moving the scissors so that they made their terrifying sound.

SKROOSH, SCREEESH, SCHROOOOSH, SCHREEEEESH.

Pearlyclaws tiptoed over to Brian's straw bed...

And...

He couldn't see Brian.

He put down the scissors and rummaged in the straw.

No Brian.

He kicked the straw with his beautiful (or so he thought) feet.

Still no Brian.

He looked all over the barn.

He couldn't see Brian anywhere.

Hooray!

But where on Earth could Brian have gone?

BILL WAKES UP! (FINALLY)

SECTION TWENTY-SIX

In which we find hat theft!

Meanwhile, down in the farmhouse Badger Bill was finally waking up. Although the Speshul Cocoa was extremely strong, he was too worried about his friends to sleep any longer.

"Oofff." He sat straight up in bed with his fur feeling frizzled and his claws tingling. "I will get a water of glass. No, a glass of water." His thoughts were as tangled as snakes in a disco. "Oh, I feel so wibbly and woozly…"

He got out of his little badger bed.

And—

Oh no! His little badger bedroom was empty!

There was no fluffy blue rug for his morning toes and no curtains and no wardrobe with his waistcoats. (Sometimes Bill wore waistcoats to look especially dashing.) There was no cupboard to hold his pullovers and no pullovers. There was no bookshelf to hold his books about famous and interesting badgers and there were no books, and no globe showing all the places in the world he wanted to go. There was no moon chart, showing when it should be bright and full and when it should be dark and new.

AND THERE WERE NO HATS!

Bill loved his hats. He had a hat for every single occasion. And every one of them had vanished!

The only thing left in his room was his bed, and someone had even slipped the sheet out from underneath his sleeping body and sneaked off with his favourite quilt – the one with the badger explorers on!

Bill's head was whirling so fast he felt as if his eyes might go googly, but the nasty surprise was beginning to clear his brain and weaken the effects of the Speshul Cocoa. "Who can have done this?" he asked himself. "And why didn't Miranda stop them?" The whirling kept on and cleared more and more of his thinking. "Miranda is beautiful and she has silky fur. She wouldn't steal everything. Would she...?"

And then all the wriggly, naggly feelings at the back of Bill's head that had been trying to warn him ever since he met Miranda came rushing in.

"She has stolen all of my things! She has stolen all of Uncle Shawn's things! She has stolen my hats!"

Bill ran through every room in the farmhouse, finding nothing but dust and dirty paw prints and marks on walls where pictures used to hang. Miranda had even taken the toilet seat. And the toilet.

Bill stamped in annoyance. "I thought I was in love with her. I thought that she was in love with me! All she did was bully me and feed me nasty cocoa and hit my ears.

Wickedenia BADGER

ENEMY OF ALL LIZARDS! MAY BITE!!!

Oh, she may be the worst badger in the world! Worse than Wickedenia Badger who once filled every post box in Hull with irritated lizards. Oh, I have been such a fool!"

Then Bill's tummy went all cold and worried. "I was supposed to look after everyone. I forgot about all my friends! Are they safe?! And what will Uncle Shawn think when he sees the farmhouse is empty? He won't like me any more and he was my best friend ever in the whole world and I will miss him! And the llamas will hate me and I will miss them too!"

Poor Bill held his head in his paws as big badger tears rolled down the stripes of his little badger nose.

"I wish I'd never seen Miranda. I wish I had gone to the moon. I wish everything would go back to the way it was." But nothing happened. His wishes weren't working.

"I need a plan," thought Bill, being very brave. "I need a Defeat Miranda Plan. Oh, but I need my friends to help me. I wonder where they are and if they still like me. And I do hope Miranda hasn't been nasty to them."

Although he still felt strange from the Speshul Cocoa, Bill stumbled off to make sure his llama pals were all right. 🐾

KING FOOM

SECTION TWENTY-SEVEN

In which we find moonfolk and – oh, thank goodness! – maybe the start of some rescuing.

Back on the moon, Uncle Shawn and Sam stared up at the vast, shadowy moon creature. Sam held his breath and waited to be thrown into a moon dungeon, or worse.

But then Sam heard Uncle Shawn laugh a huge laugh and call out, "King Foom, how wonderful to see you again!"

The tall moon creature clapped its foggy hands together and chuckled with a sound like thunder. "Uncle Shawn! How excellent to see you. My people – the proud and magnificent Hurrfoofurrhurrs – thought you were spies from those dreadful Paafoofurrhurrs. They are our enemies forever now, their queen is a terrible person and I don't know why I liked her. And I don't miss all the games we used to play. Or our banquets. Or the hat-making and fun.

But now we each have to keep on opposite sides of the border so all the light is in the wrong place and the moon doesn't sing any more." He sighed. "I suppose we will be at war and do war-type things – once we can work out how."

King Foom shook his foggy fist and the other Hurrfoofurrhurrs growled. They sounded like sleepy bees, which wasn't very scary, but Uncle Shawn thought to himself, "Hmmmm. If the moon people work out how to fight each other properly, lots of them could get hurt. This is not good at all. I thought I would have got a big, shiny wish for Sky by now and be on my way home... And where is

KING FOOM'S
WAR PLANS

1. NO MORE HATS
2. NO MORE GAMES
3. NO MORE TICKLING
4. NO MORE SENDING
   BIRTHDAY CARDS
5. ERM... THAT'S IT

Sky? And where is my magnet? And how long will our powdered air last? I didn't bring enough for a long visit." Uncle Shawn rubbed his hand through his wibbly hair. "This moon trip could either be a wonderful adventure, or a big mistake." He tried whistling to keep himself cheery. Then he stopped in case it wasted too much air.

But then he noticed marks appearing in the

moon dust near his feet. It was almost as if someone was writing with an invisible finger...

S

K

Y

And he grinned a gigantunormous Uncle Shawn
grin and thought, "My, my. Well, I think I might
enjoy being rescued by a clever invisible girl." And
he winked at nothing at all.

And the patch of nothing at all giggled as if it
were a brave and resourceful girl.

• • •

Just as Uncle Shawn was thinking, "I hope Brian
isn't too worried that we have been away so long,"
Sylvester Pearlyclaws was searching for Brian
in every barn and shed and strawberry patch,

kicking at piles of leaves and generally being furious. He had left his big scissors in Brian's barn because they were so heavy. But this didn't mean he had forgotten about nose snipping.

But where was Brian? How did he escape from the barn without Pearlyclaws seeing him? Did he wish very hard and become an invisible llama?

No, he can't have – nobody's wishes are working!

Well, in fact ... Brian was still in the barn!

As soon as Claude heard Pearlyclaws' plan he

had sent a coded signal of tugs and taps along the thin thread all spiders use to keep in touch. (They call it the World Wide Web.)

This meant that hundreds of spiders had rushed to help Claude. Together they had woven a spiderweb hammock, big enough to hold Brian.

The spiders wrapped Brian up in it at amazing speed, so Brian suddenly found himself covered in sticky spiderweb.

Shouting "Heave!" in their tiny spider voices, they hauled Brian up into the barn's rafters and stuck him to the beams with extra gluey threads.

This was very strange and scary for Brian, but Claude stood just inside one of his elegant ears and whispered, "Be really still, Brian, and don't make a sound. We will look after you. Don't think about hundreds of spiders running up and down all over you."

Naturally, this did make Brian think of hundreds of spiders running up and down all over him, so his fur stood up as if he had been struck by lightning while getting a perm. This made the

spider threads stick to him even more and helped him stay safely on the ceiling when Pearlyclaws burst in and started searching for him. Pearlyclaws never looked up because he knew that llamas can't fly or climb up onto roof beams.

Brian and the spiders didn't make a sound and stayed perfectly still. (Brian couldn't have moved if he'd wanted to.) After what seemed like years and years, Pearlyclaws had stormed away.

This allowed the spiders to scamper down and cover the scissors in web. The metal was too heavy for them to lift, but they did manage to glue the blades firmly to the floor.

After that, the spiders all cheered. Then they swung back and forth on spider trapezes and sang their anthem:

The World Association
For the spiders of every nation
We sway, we swing
We swoop, we sing
Eight great feet
With a spider beat
We help and save

And are mostly brave
Yes! The Spider Association!

And after that, the spiders rested, hanging comfortably upside down, or tucking themselves into cracks and corners.

Outside was the crashing of Pearlyclaws searching the farm with growls and kicks.

Inside was the muffled and sticky voice of a llama with thread wrapped round his mouth.

"Excufe me, pleafe. May I met mown now?"

Brian was asking if he could get down now.

He was stuck firmly to the ceiling and that meant he was safe, but how could Brian save his friends when he was covered in web? And if the spiders unstuck him, wouldn't he just fall onto the hard floor of the barn? Brian had knee pads and a parachute and all kinds of other safety equipment – but they were out of reach, safe inside his Safety Cupboard Number Three.

Brian sighed, "I will be very sore if I do hit the floor." That rhymed, but it didn't make Brian smile.

SECTION TWENTY-EIGHT

In which we find Miranda's cave. Don't touch anything – it will all be sticky and grimy and covered in soot and wickedness. This section also explains how Miranda and Pearlyclaws met. In case you were wondering.

Miranda Badger was back in the nasty, smoky den which had never really been her home. She was wearing tough, practical overalls and a big tool belt, because she was no longer pretending to be pretty. She had a lot of work to do, lifting and carrying and pushing.

And what was she lifting and carrying and

MIRANDA'S EVIL HOBBIES

① HIDING DOG POO IN SHOPPING BAGS

shoppe

squirrel provisions

② EVIL PLUMBING

③ EVIL CARPENTRY

④ TEASING SHARKS

⑤ STEALING BONNETS

⑥ STEALING EVERY-THING ELSE

SWAG

⑦ UPSETTING POOR BILL

pushing? Everything she'd taken from the farm-house – including all the kitchen tiles and the doorknobs and the doors!

Miranda had always liked being wicked: stealing watches and bicycles, punching people in queues, slipping dog poo into people's shopping bags and generally making sure everyone she met became as unhappy as possible. But she dreamed of being truly dreadful, a famously bad badger. She wanted people to write nursery rhymes about her and to put up Wanted posters showing her picture (taken from the left, which was her best side).

A few weeks before she met Bill, Miranda had been walking along a pebbly beach, bored and sad that there was no one around to kick or call names. Then she had seen a strange bottle glimmering on the sand.

She hoped it contained a genie to grant her some terrible wishes, but instead it contained a letter that was almost as good.

Or bad – depending on whether you're an awful badger or not.

Dear Reader,

If you are reelly wicked, wait for me in Shoogeldy Bay until I escape my current prison which is a whale's stomach. (Excuse the smell.)

I will then help you with speshul poshuns of great power and help you steal things. Then you can be comfurtubble while you are being horribull.

And you can help me to destroy all the friends of Uncle Shawn, the most stupid, kind and happy man on Earth. We will destroy him until he is nuffink but a puddle of tears and maybe one shoe.

I am lauffing in a very evil way rite now.

If you are not wicked, please ignore this note.

Yours Since Really,

Sylvester Pearlyclaws – Master Crinimal

Pearlyclaws couldn't spell and had no computer to help him inside the whale. And it took him ages to tickle the whale enough to spit out the bottle, so that someone would be ready to help him do disgusting and wicked things as soon as he escaped.

Miranda had waited for him and plotted with him and given his Speshul Cocoa to poor Bill. Now her den was full of everything from the farmhouse. The toilet was sitting in a corner like a disconnected throne, and Bill's favourite quilt was all screwed up on the dirty floor. Miranda looked at her spoils and rubbed her paws together.

PILE OF BILL'S AND
UNCLE SHAWN'S
THINGS

"While Bill is full of Speshul Cocoa I will feed him Truth Potion and ask him about the hidden treasure that Uncle Shawn must have. Then I will steal it before Pearlyclaws can and then I will sell all this and he'll get nothing." Miranda wiggled her tail with glee.

That's the trouble with being wicked and joining forces with other wicked people – you will probably be wicked to each other, as well.

Miranda hadn't been able to find any treasure in the farmhouse (because it wasn't there), and now she was furious. "That stupid, fat-legged badger better know where the treasure is," she growled as she stamped about between stolen ornaments and stolen furniture. "I can't dig up the whole farm – it would take weeks and ruin my pretty complexion."

Her complexion was as pretty as a fish processing plant, but – as you know – liars lie to everyone, even themselves. 🐾

RUNNING TO THE RESCUE

SECTION TWENTY-NINE

In which Bill is feeling much better! Hooray! But this section also contains an EMEMENCIA. And so it should probably also contain a Great Big Plan.

I hope someone has one.

Back on the farm, Bill headed for Brian's barn, because he thought he should check on his most nervous friend first.

It looked like the barn was empty, but then Bill heard a strange sound that stopped him.

"Ememencia! Bim Ememencia!"

"Hmm," thought Bill. "It sounds as if Brian has his mouth full of toffee and is floating above me. But that's impossible."

But Bill looked up at the ceiling and there was Brian! All wrapped in web! And there, also, were hundreds and hundreds of very friendly but very spidery spiders.

"Aaaah!" yelped Bill. "What are you doing to Brian? Leave him alone, he is a wonderful, brave, lovely llama!"

This made Brian feel proud and happy and he wiggled his bottom in its silky trousers, because that was the only way he could say thank you.

Claude quickly bounced down on a thread and whispered in his spidery, tiny voice, "We were helping. We hid him in the ceiling, but now we can't get him down again. Please help us."

Bill was still a bit woozy. He thought of the problem of Brian stuck on the ceiling and the problem of strong sticky sheets of spider threads and the problem of Miranda and the problem of having no furniture and...

There were just so many problems!

But then, Bill's clever badger face broke into a huge smile. "I think I have a plan!" All the excitement was shaking the last of the Speshul Cocoa out of his brain and, if he'd had time, he would have done the Dance of Badger Delight.

THE DANCE OF BADGER DELIGHT

"I think I have a plan so amazing that even Uncle Shawn would feel proud of it." Bill stood up straight and tall and seemed to be almost back to his usual self. "I will push Brian's straw bed right underneath him and then you spiders can gently release all of your threads."

Brian tried to say, "That could go wrong, Señor Bill!" But the sticky web made it sound much more like, "Mat mood mow wong, Menor Mill!" So nobody understood.

"It's all right Brian!" called Bill. "Be brave! And when you're on the ground I will tell you about my plan. It's a Great Big Plan to Defeat a Big Emergencia."

Bill was so impressive that Brian stopped wriggling and feeling scared. This meant that the spiders could tickle him free of all the web and then help Bill slowly lower him to the floor. Brian even felt well enough to say, "Thank you, Señor and Señora Spiders. Gracias."

SHADOWY PUDDING

SECTION THIRTY

In which we are running out of air! Oh no!

Sam thought the Hurrfoofurrhurrs were nice, even though they were keeping him and Uncle Shawn prisoner on the moon in case the terrible war started and they got hurt. One called Noof gave Sam and Uncle Shawn a big bowl of pudding which looked like the kind of shadow you'd find under a tree, but tasted like chocolate.

Uncle Shawn said, "Thank you very much." Then he tickled Noof's feet.

Sam thought this was rather strange.

"The Hurrfoofurrhurrs love being tickled,"

explained Uncle Shawn. "For them it's sort of the same as money. They and the Paafoofurrhurrs used to tickle and play and dance and sing every day, then gather up the wish energy from the Earth and make the best ones come true and make whatever was left over into the most marvellous hats in the whole universe. Everyone on the moon would get together on holidays and hold the Ceremony of the Hats and all swap hats and tickles. They used to have so much fun and be so happy." He sighed. But then he nodded and concentrated on his plan. "Tickling is a really good way to distract the Hurrfoofurrhurrs while an invisible person is creeping about and doesn't want to be caught leaving footprints in the moon dust."

As Uncle Shawn spoke, Sam saw small footprints in the moon dust being swiped away, as if by invisible feet.

"Do you have a plan?" whispered Sam.

"Weeell..." Uncle Shawn whispered back.

HOW TO PERFORM THE CEREMONY OF THE HATS

1 GET NICE HAT

2 GO AND FACE YOUR NEW FRIEND WHO ALSO HAS A NICE HAT

3 BOW POLITELY

4 SAY:

Blingy-Plingy-wufflebuffle-floom

(WITHOUT LAUGHING)

5 SWAP HATS

6 DO THE WRIGGLE OF JOY

7 ADMIRE YOUR NEW HAT AND DANCE LIKE A HAPPY BADGER!

"Maybe I do. Please keep the other Hurrfoo-furrhurrs busy here. Tickle them as if your life depends on it. It just might. If you can tickle them enough, they will fall asleep and you will be able to escape to talk to Queen Wufflebuffle of the Paafoofurrhurrs and try to get her to come to a Ceremony of the Hats one last time..." He whispered a bit more of his plan into Sam's ear so that

no one could hear it, not even us. Then he laughed and said, "And now I have to speak to King Foom." While Sam was tickling as he had never tickled before, Uncle Shawn joined Foom, King of the Hurrfoofurrhurrs, in a foggy misty garden with shadowy blue and black trees and murky flowers.

Uncle Shawn began, "Surely if you were such good friends with all the Paafoofurrhurrs, why can't you just all say sorry and start playing games and granting wishes and making hats again?"

"Never," sighed Foom. "Even if we forgave them for whatever it was they did, they would never forgive us for whatever it was we did. I just know it. That queen of theirs would never forgive

me, even if she is very nice and sweet and lovely."

"Have you asked her?"

"Of course not. You don't understand, Uncle Shawn. This is terrible, but we can't do anything about it."

Uncle Shawn looked down at the moon dust

behind Foom. He could see the imprints of two feet which had followed him outside very quietly. He began to speak extra loudly and clearly, almost as if he was making sure someone called Sky understood his plan. "Well, King Foom. Before you begin to have a proper war, I think you should hold one last Ceremony of the Hats. Call the Hurrfoofurrhurrs together. Then Queen Wufflebuffle and her people can meet you and your people, the way you always used to."

"Oh, she'd never agree to do that," said Foom.

"We'll see," said Uncle Shawn and he grinned at the empty space where someone invisible was standing. "Then you can give each other hats, the way you always did, just one last time."

Uncle Shawn rubbed his wibbly hair and hoped that his Save The Moon Plan was going to work before they all ran out of powdered air... 🐾

BADGER SLIPPERS!
EEEK!

SECTION THIRTY-ONE

In which we find... Oh, dear –

A MONSTER! EMERGENCIA!!!

Bill was whispering to Brian in the dark, "I'm sure this will be all right."

Brian whispered back, "I do hope so."

They tightened their knee pads and adjusted their life jackets, even though they weren't at all sure they would help.

Through the hedge, they could hear Pearlyclaws kicking at lumps of grass and threatening rabbits and grinding his huge teeth. "Lazy, lily-livered llamas! Disappearing to annoy me! Blithering blasted badger! I won't just ask him about buried treasure, I'll scoop out his insides and make him into slippers!" Pearlyclaws was so annoyed he pulled off his false moustache and threw it away. Bill and Brian watched it flop over the hedge and land unpleasantly at their feet.

"That cowardly llama! I'll have his nose if it's the last nose I snip and then I'll laugh at him and he will cry!" raged Pearlyclaws. "I'll have my revenge on all of them, or my name isn't Sylvester Pearlyclaws!"

"Oh, no!" whispered Bill. "It really is Sylvester Pearlyclaws! I hoped we had got rid of him forever."

"This is a bigger Emergencia than we can deal with. I don't think we will succeed," mumbled Brian.

But then...

Many completely horrifying things took place.

Look away now, or lie down and hold on to your blanket.

PEARLYCLAWS REVEALED!

EMERGENCIA!

BIGGER EMERGENCIA!

SIDNEY SMITH   SYLVESTER PEARLYCLAWS

As Bill and Brian trembled and Pearlyclaws rampaged across the grass and young rabbits bounced in all directions, the hedge at the corner of the meadow swayed and swelled and then—

AAAAAAAAAAAAAAAAAAAAAAAAAGH!

A giant spider that was taller than a set of steps burst through the leaves and twigs and hissed and coughed and squeaked and wobbled

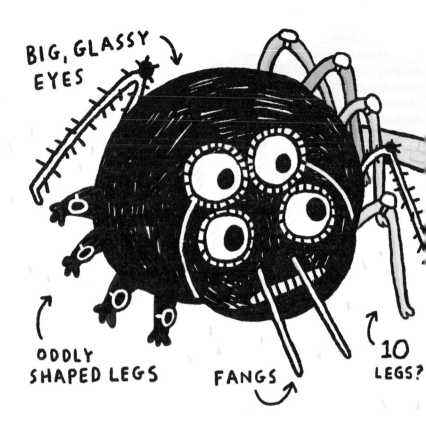

BIG, GLASSY EYES

ODDLY SHAPED LEGS

FANGS

10 LEGS?

four of its enormous sticky hairy legs, and trotted forward on another six of its (we would have to say) rather oddly shaped legs.

That made ten legs! A spider with ten legs must be the worst possible kind!

Spiders were the only thing that scared Pearlyclaws. Even being swallowed by a whale

HUGE HORSE
TEETH

– and then being vomited out of a whale – had only made him a bit more annoyed than usual.

And this was a seven-foot tall, wobbly spider with knobbly knees! And it was chasing him!

Pearlyclaws was so frightened that his huge horse teeth flew out of his mouth, twirled in mid-air, bounced over a wall, rolled down a slope and finally ended up in the field where a very elderly horse called Patricia lived. She had lost her false teeth and couldn't remember where. (She had taken them out and left them on a table when she was visiting a friend in the Horse Hospital and wanted to eat a hard toffee.)

She spotted these teeth with a pleased snort, tried them on and found they were a perfect fit. (In fact, they were hers.) Patricia wore them proudly for the rest of her life. Losing his teeth was the only good thing Pearlyclaws ever did for anyone.

PATRICIA
THE HORSE

Back on the farm, Pearlyclaws didn't care a bit about having a gumsy mouth. He felt sick. This was his worst nightmare, come to life – a giant, angry spider. (And he had a feeling that some-where a horse was very happy – that gave him a pain worse than indigestion.)

"Grrrrrrr. I am the Emperor of Spiders!" screeched the massive spider, waving what seemed to be two massive fangs in the air and staring at him through four big glassy eyes.

Pearlyclaws tried to shout, "No, no. Please spare me. I won't do it again – whatever it was I did." Without his teeth, it was, "Mo, mo. Mease smare me! I mon't moo it amain – matever it mas mad I did." Although he liked to seem fearless and strong, he was actually a complete scaredy-cat. "Meeeze!"

Then the Spider Emperor's voice changed and sounded a bit Peruvian as it shouted, "You are cruel and wrong to everyone you meet. I will not stand for it!" The spider stood still and looked very impressive and some of its legs wriggled in a way that would have made you scream. "Leave now, or I will bite you with my fangs!"

Pearlyclaws shouted a toothless version of, "Oh, no. No biting!"

The monster rattled its fangs together so that they sounded like angry knitting needles and yelled, "*¡Soy el Emperador de las Arañas! ¡Huir!*", which meant "I am the Emperor of Spiders! Run away!" in Spanish.

And Pearlyclaws ran away so fast you might have expected his trousers to catch fire.

While we wonder why that terrifying spider was speaking in English and Spanish and had fangs just like knitting needles, we must go back up to the moon. 🐾

MILKY-WAY MILKSHAKE

SECTION THIRTY-TWO

In which Sam is very clever and brave.

Just as Uncle Shawn had planned, Sam tickled his Hurrfoofurrhurr guards until they fell into a happy, giggly sleep. Then he crept away and quickly crossed the border into Paafoofurrhurr territory. It wasn't long before sentries caught him and took him just where he wanted to be – right inside the palace of Queen Wufflebuffle.

Sam had thought the sentries were shiny and sparkly and bright, but when the queen swept into her Hall of Examining Visitors, she was too bright to look at. If you had squashed the Milky

Way into a milkshake it might have looked as dazzling as Wufflebuffle.

"Please, Your Worshipful Majesty," said Sam,"King Foom would like you to do the Ceremony of the Hats one last time."

"That's a completely stupid idea," Wufflebuffle said in a voice like xylophones and the little bells on the collars of a thousand cats. "Just like him to be so stupid."

"Ah, but how clever of you it would be to take all your finest hats and make the Hurrfoofurrhurrs ashamed of theirs."

"I won't go!" Wufflebuffle stamped her foot with a shower of sparks like a furnace with indigestion.

Sam was very clever and knew what to say next. "Oh, well. Foom did tell me that you wouldn't want to come because you were the most stubborn person he'd ever met."

"Me?!" This sounded like milk bottles crashing down a mountain. "Me?! Stubborn?! I could show him – the silly fat face – I could just go to the border at once and be there before him. And all my people would bring the finest hats the universe has ever seen and he would be very impressed. I could do that now, if I really wanted."

Sam tried not to giggle – he had nearly persuaded her. It would just take a little more work...

"Foom's the one who's stubborn." Wufflebuffle peered at Sam with her glimmering eyes. "Come and have some pudding."

She gripped Sam's hand with her sparkling fingers and walked him along to the kitchen. "I'm sure you must be starving. Hurrfoofurrhurr cooking is terrible. You don't like being tickled, do you?" She sighed. "I do miss tickling the Hurrfoofurrhurrs.

And I liked playing games with them. We all did. And I quite liked looking at King Foom's silly big misty face..." She sighed again.

"I quite like being tickled," said Sam, and then he added cleverly, "I'd be happy to let you tickle me, but I'm only one very small boy. I bet it would be much better to get everyone on the moon together in one place: the Hurrfoofurrhurrs – who like being tickled – and all your people – who like tickling. And maybe you could swap some hats..."

The queen looked at him sharply, as if she suspected he might be trying to make her part of a great big gigantunormous plan to save the moon. But then she wriggled her sparkly fingers and giggled like bicycle bells. "First I shall practise tickling on you, young Earth person, and then I shall think... I suppose it wouldn't be too horrible to have to see that stupid, stubborn king again. Maybe..." She smiled a far-away kind of smile. 🐾

TERRIFYING SPIDER FANGS

SECTION THIRTY-THREE

In which there is a not very frightening monster
and lots of extremely useful safety equipment.

Back on the farm, as you may have guessed, Brian and Bill were hugging and congratulating each other on having done so well at pretending to be a giant spider.

After Brian had been freed from the spiderweb that was holding him on the ceiling, he and Bill had made a spider suit out of sticky web. They constructed a pair of wobbly spider arms out of more web and borrowed a pair of Guinevere's knitting needles to use as fangs. They had worn two of Brian's gas masks to give themselves strange eyes, and worn knee pads to make their knees knobbly. Then they had hissed and shouted and waved their false arms and trotted about on llama legs and badger legs. (That's why the spider had two more legs than it ought to.)

Both our friends were really sticky and hot inside the spider costume, but they were sure they had defeated Pearlyclaws.

And Brian knew he had been very, very brave, because Bill told him so. "You were so fierce and wonderful." Bill hugged Brian again. "This was much more fun than being in love and letting Miranda biff my ears." He took off his gas mask because it was so hot.

"I hope Guinevere does not mind that I made her knitting come undone," worried Brian, removing his mask. "Where is she? And where are Carlos and Ginalolobrigida? Oooh … I have a worried feeling in my tummy and it is spreading to my ears."

"Oh, but I wonder where Miranda is," Bill said. "She's such a terrible badger. And where is everything from the farmhouse? And where are my hats?! She stole it all, you know! And what if she is being nasty to the llamas?! If anyone could manage to be nasty to a wonderful animal like a llama it would be her."

THINGS MORE FUN THAN BEING IN LOVE WITH MIRANDA

HAVING YOUR EARS TWISTED

WATCHING PAINT DRY

DOING LONG SUMS

JUGGLING WASPS

"Do not worry, Bill." Brian rubbed Bill's shoulder with his big llama nose that no one had snipped. He had decided to keep on being brave until everyone was safe. "We will go and be a spider at her and she will run away, too. And we will find Carlos and Ginalolobrigida and Guinevere and then we will have lemonade and hugs."

Brian smiled. Bravely.

THE MOON BEHAVING STRANGELY

SECTION THIRTY-FOUR

In which we find Uncle Shawn and
a moon full of hats. And Uncle Shawn's
Save The Moon Plan! I hope it works!

All of the Hurrfoofurrhurrs and Paafoofurrhurrs were milling about at the border on the moon.

Astronomers in Australia (where it was night) were looking through their telescopes and noticed the moon behaving very strangely. The bright parts and the shadowy parts were jiggling about. Some parts were really too dark, some parts were really too bright, and some were just dusty and a bit boring in ways that weren't quite right.

We know what was really happening, but the astronomers had to shake their heads and puzzle over their big books about the moon. Then they went and had a cup of tea and hoped it would all have gone back to normal when they looked again.

CONFUSED ASTRONOMERS

Uncle Shawn held Sam's hand and smiled a secret smile and felt Sky's invisible hand hold his and knew that soon he would be able to make all kinds of wishes. And so would everyone on Earth.

The Paafoofurrhurrs and Hurrfoofurrhurrs

were keeping a little bit apart because they were at war. But some of them were also waving and shouting to friends and hugging a little bit, because they had missed seeing them. Foom and Wufflebuffle were facing each other and trying not to be happy.

Uncle Shawn walked towards them with his arms held wide, scuffling his feet a lot in the dust so that no one would notice any footprints from invisible feet. "And now," yelled Uncle Shawn, sounding very official, "the exchanging of the hats."

All the moonfolk had brought their hats with them and some of them giggled and clapped, because the only thing better than making a wonderful hat is giving it to someone. The tassels on the Hurrfoofurrhurrs' hats waved as they waggled them and the sequins glittered. The ribbons and bows on the Paafoofurrhurrs' hats also waved and the tinsel on their brims looked very fine.

Then Uncle Shawn announced in a great, loud voice that could almost be heard on Earth, "King Foom and Queen Wufflebuffle will exchange hats first. Then you will all exchange hats. And we shall see what we shall see!"

The king and queen stared at each other, Foom's shadow eyebrows looking very stern and the glittering of Wufflebuffle's hair showering everyone in sparks. They held out their extraordinary hats, which were highly impressive and covered in bells and jewels and sweets in pretty wrappers. But then they did nothing except stare some more.

"What's wrong?" asked Uncle Shawn.

Wufflebuffle hissed, "We didn't start this, so they should hand over the first hat."

Foom growled, "Well, we didn't start this either, so they should hand over the first hat."

Uncle Shawn's eyes sparkled and he said quietly, "Well, if you're going to be annoyed, you should just put your hats on the ground and turn your backs on each other." He chuckled and waved his hands in a way that seemed a little bit like waving to an invisible girl.

Once the hats were resting on the ground and their owners had their backs turned, Wufflebuffle's hat floated away from her and then Foom's hat quietly floated away from him.

Then, while every single moon person watched, even the babies, Foom's hat landed on Wufflebuffle's head and Wufflebuffle's hat landed on Foom's head – just as if an invisible girl had helped them to be more sensible.

As soon as the hats settled on their heads, Foom and Wufflebuffle turned round and looked at each other. Then they both said, "Thank you."

And then they both laughed.

After that they hugged each other and both shouted, "I knew you'd see sense!" Then they both laughed again and said, "No, I knew *you'd* see sense!" And then they were quieter and said together, "And I knew I'd see sense, too." And then they hugged some more.

The Paafoofurrhurrs and Hurrfoofurrhurrs had been watching everything, holding their breath. Now they all cheered and hugged everyone they could reach and gave hats and swapped hats and even threw hats in the air.

Down on Earth the astronomers, who had just come back from their cups of tea, looked through their telescopes and saw the strange lights and shadows caused by this and had to lie down and have even more tea and some biscuits. Some of them gave up being astronomers and started to grow carrots instead.

EVEN MORE ↗
CONFUSED ASTRONOMERS

But what about the wishes? Can we make wishes yet?! We really need them now! 🐾

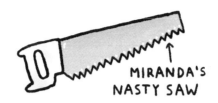

MIRANDA'S
NASTY SAW

SECTION THIRTY-FIVE

*In which I really wish we could wish, because
things aren't going to turn out quite as well
as we were hoping. There are lovely animals
with beautiful noses in danger and some of
them have been hypnotised! Oh no!*

Pearlyclaws had run on his precious feet like an evil egg away from Bill and Brian and – MASH – crashed into Miranda, who was looking for Bill.

"Ooff..." said Miranda as she was knocked onto her big bottom.

Pearlyclaws glared at Miranda. With his

gummy mouth he told her, "Ooo look werry ugly in oweralls."

"Why weren't you looking where you were going?" said Miranda. "And where are your teeth? And your moustache? Without your hat you look like an angry egg."

"Oo oook uglier!" yelled Pearlyclaws. And also, "SPIDDDDEER!" He mimed being chased by a giant spider while Miranda laughed.

"What nonsense. You've been drinking one of your own potions." She thumped him with one of her meaty paws. "I don't think there's any treasure here and I can't find Bill. Let's just snip off as many noses as we can and then leave. When Uncle Shawn is back from the moon and you've got some teeth, you can think of a better plan."

"Mut whad about da spider?"

"I don't believe there ever was a spider. I bet you've snipped off all the noses and you're trying to cheat me."

"No. We gan snip dem now," said Pearlyclaws.

Miranda wiggled her tail with joy. "Yes. Let's snip them now. Where are your big scissors? I suppose you have lost them. Well, we can use the saw in my tool belt." Miranda chuckled a terrible chuckle.

Then – oh, goodness and dearie, dearie me – both those horrible creatures walked back towards the llamas who were sleeping peacefully in the meadow!

Oh, NO!

SLEEPING LLAMAS

Still deep under the spell of Pearlyclaws' hypnotism, Ginalolobrigida was snoozing and Carlos was snoring and Guinevere was dozing. They looked so peaceful and happy and calm.

And they didn't have any idea that Pearlyclaws and Miranda were RIGHT IN FRONT OF THEM!

Pearlyclaws was smiling as much as anyone can with no teeth and staring at the llamas wonderful noses as if they were ripe apples he was going to pick.

Miranda was sharpening her saw on a stone to make it even nastier...

Oh, no!

Can we bear to look?

Goodness me!

Miranda Badger was now waving her saw in the air and enjoying the way it glittered. She was sure it was exactly sharp enough to slice poor, defenceless noses easily and smoothly so that her arm wouldn't get tired. "You hold up their silly heads and I will get sawing," she growled.

But, exactly at that moment, that terrible huge spider battered through the hedge.

"Leave those llamas alone!" it shrieked.

Pearlyclaws quickly hid behind Miranda and shrieked back, "Noooo!"

Miranda jumped back too and both the nasty badger and the international criminal called Pearlyclaws started to run away.

Phew!

But then...

Miranda stopped. "Hang on a minute. I recognise that stupid, fat voice," she sneered.

She turned round and examined the spider costume, which wasn't quite as good and convincing as it had been. One of its wibbly arms had been pulled off by the hedge, and the knitting needles had dropped out of Bill's paws because he was hot and all of him was sweating a lot. Some of the knee pads had come loose and were looking a bit sad.

Miranda grabbed Pearlyclaws by his collar and dragged him back towards the spider, and even though it shouted, "Beware of the huge spider! *¡Si! ¡Ten cuidado con la enorme araña!*" Miranda kicked its front legs (which belonged to Bill) and snorted down her nose in a very unladylike way.

"It's that idiot badger and that cowardly llama. We can take care of them."

And while Bill's fur and Brian's fur went all shivery with fright and they wished they hadn't taken off their gas masks (because they covered their noses), Miranda closed in on them, and Pearlyclaws kicked Carlos' leg because no one could stop him.

Pearlyclaws chuckled. "More noses to snip. We can deal with every single one of Uncle Shawn's animal friends here at once. Perfect. Then we'll just wait for him and the twins. And while we are waiting we can think up new terrible things we can do to them."

And he and Miranda held hands and did the ugliest dance the universe has ever seen. 🐾

**VERY SMALL
PILE OF POWDERED
AIR**

SECTION THIRTY-SIX

*In which perhaps Uncle Shawn and Sam and invisible
Sky will run out of air before they manage to mend
everybody's wishes on Earth and get home! Maybe
we should all wish that everything turns out happily
for everyone – and hope our wishes can work now.*

Up on the moon, Uncle Shawn was having to
shout above all the sounds of happiness and jingling bells and tickling and enjoyment. His Save
The Moon Plan had worked and he had stopped
the moon going to war. But he still had to get
all the way home with the twins. He could tell
they were both worried about not being able to

breathe for much longer. "I am afraid we have to go now and we need our magnet back so that we can make our dish fly, dear moon people," he said to the big crowd around him. "It has been nice to see you, but I think we need to hurry."

As soon as they remembered Uncle Shawn and Sam were there, Queen Wufflebuffle and King Foom rushed in and tickled them and picked them up and held them in the air. They both shouted, "Uncle Shawn, you are a very clever and wonderful man! And well done Sam!" Of course, they couldn't see Sky.

"This is very nice, but please let us go," called Uncle Shawn, as his long arms and lanky legs jiggled in the air and he looked across at Sam. "And we really will need our big magnet and our big metal dish and – oh – lots of wishes and quite a few hats."

Foom laughed. "Of course. The moon will be able to catch and grant wishes again now we are

all happy. And you can have your magnet back!"
He started to tickle Wufflebuffle and she tickled
Pinginging and she tickled Noof and he started to
tickle Pappaboo.

"Oh dear," thought Sky. "Tickling is nice
sometimes, but not right now. We're going to run
out of air!"

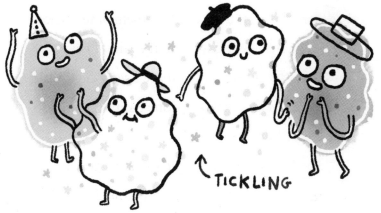

TICKLING

Soon everyone was tickling everyone else and
so many moon people were tickling Nif that he
hiccupped and hiccoughed and then – up came
the magnet in a blaze of blue sparks. Nif didn't
need it any more to make himself feel tickly.
Everybody cheered.

Some Paafoofurrhurrs and Hurrfoofurrhurrs brought over the big metal dish, running on their sparkly and shadowy feet, and it wasn't long before Sam and Uncle Shawn and – secretly – Sky were standing ready on the thrumming metal surface, waiting to fly.

The Hurrfoofurrhurrs waved and the Paafoofurrhurrs waved and Foom and Wufflebuffle shook Uncle Shawn's hand and bowed to Sam, who was thinking, "I don't know if I can hold my breath all the way back to Earth – it took us so long to get here. We don't have enough powdered air left..."

"How did you get us to be friends again?" Wufflebuffle asked Uncle Shawn, just when he thought they could get away.

"Yes, I think you're a little bit magic," Foom chuckled.

"Oh, I had the help of my friends. Having friends always makes everyone a little bit magic." Uncle Shawn smiled, and everyone heard the giggle of an invisible little girl. They watched as Uncle Shawn reached out and held Sam's hand to his right, and then reached out and seemed to take hold of an invisible hand to his left. Uncle Shawn winked and his hair wiggled happily.

"I see..." Foom laughed. "Or rather, I don't see at all."

"Thank you so much for helping us," sparkled Wufflebuffle.

"I don't know why we were being so silly," rumbled Foom and he reached out his cloudy hand to Wufflebuffle's light-filled hand. "We love each other really." When he realised he had said that out loud, his cloudy head and hands and body all turned a strange sort of pink – as if the sun was setting behind rainclouds.

And Wufflebuffle's lights also became all shades of red, pinks and purples.

"I think we should leave you two to be happily in love," said Uncle Shawn, feeling a bit short of breath.

Both the royal moonfolk blushed even more colourfully.

Moonfolk rushed in again from all directions and gave Uncle Shawn the moon's finest hats and tickled his elbows gently as a thank you, because they had never wanted to be at war and were so happy now that they could run and play tag and make more hats and have all the fun they could imagine with each other. They really wanted Uncle Shawn to stay with them, because he was always fun.

"I'm afraid that we have to get home to our other friends," said Uncle Shawn firmly. There was now a good-sized hill of hats around his feet. The moonfolk were being very generous.

A GOOD SIZED HILL OF HATS ↘

"Bill is down on Earth having to be in love in a really unhappy way, and goodness knows what

MOON A SHORT DISTANCE

might have happened to the llamas, and Brian does worry ... and ... air." He coughed and nodded and waved and with that he threw the big magnet up towards the earth. The iron dish spun upwards after it, just the way that a cat would chase a ball of wool and, once again, the moon rang with cheers and bells and jingling.

As the dish jumped higher and higher, the twins cheered too, and hugged. They tried to take only tiny breaths and then gasped when they saw the fresh swirling rainbow haze of new wishes and happiness and extra happiness beginning to form around the moon like the shine on a pearl.

A TERRIBLY LONG WAY TO GO

EARTH

"Well, that's all right, then." Uncle Shawn smiled. "Oh, but we still have a terribly long way to go until we're home and I have no more powdered air in my pockets. Do you, Sam? Do you, Sky?" He tried to make his voice sound worried, even though his eyes were twinkling and sparkling.

Sam scrabbled in his pockets and Sky – who had climbed back into the warm space clothes she had left in the dish – had no air either. She had held all her powder in her hand while she was being invisible, but her hand was quite empty now. There wasn't a speck of powder anywhere.

"Oh, no!" said Sam.

Sky was about to say exactly the same, but then she caught sight of Uncle Shawn's happy eyes and noticed the way that his smile was growing and growing. "Oh, but I know! We can wish for some more!"

Together they all closed their eyes and wished, and heard the loud jingling of their wish going to the moon, and saw the sparkle of it joining the growing wish cloud and making all the hats they had been given shiver with excitement (because they were wishing hats and woven out of granted wishes). And, sure enough, suddenly the iron dish was filled, not just with hats, but with enough powdered air to last for hundreds of moon trips.

"Hoorah!" they all yelled and then breathed in big gulps of new air, just because they could.

"And now, Sky, if you would like to stop being invisible, all you have to do is wish."

"Are you sure, Uncle Shawn?"

"Oh, yes. I am as sure of that as I am sure there is a fish tree in the sea." Uncle Shawn reached out his hand and wriggled his fingers so that Sky would hold it, and her brother held her other hand.

"Sky, if you would like to be visible then just try wishing. As long as you are sure you want your brother to be able to see you when you pinch him, and you want people to notice when you sneak a bite of their scones. And if you fart next to somebody they will probably know that it's you."

Sky thought about all this, but she really did want to be visible again. "I'll try."

"Good. Remember that you will be a bit older

than when you last saw yourself. And maybe your hair will need cutting. We will wish with you."

"Yes, we will," said Sam.

Together they wished and wished as the dish spun up and away from the moon and Uncle Shawn caught the magnet and threw the magnet and bounced and boonced and beenced them towards home.

Our three friends' wishes mixed together and were so powerful, and made the moon sing so loudly, that they surprised a small, young comet and made it completely change direction. The comet rushed sideways, slid right along the surface of the moon – knocking off some hats as it went – and then whizzed and plummeted towards the Earth, faster and faster.

Uncle Shawn and the twins watched as it fell and they fell more slowly and bouncily behind it.

Then they looked back at each other, and there was Uncle Shawn with his wibbly hair and his blue eyes, and there was Sam with his dirty knees and his big pullover, and THERE WAS SKY!

There was a lovely young girl – who did have very long and tangled hair. She had eyes like her brother's that sparkled nearly as brightly as Wufflebuffle's, and a friendly smile and long arms to hug her brother and then Uncle Shawn and then her brother again.

"Why are you crying, Sky?" asked Sam.

And because Sky kept on crying, Uncle Shawn answered for her. "Sometimes people cry when they are very happy, not just when they are very sad."

The cloud of happiness and granted-wish magic raced towards Earth. It whizzed and fizzed far beyond the iron dish and caught up with the comet and made it whizz and fizz even faster.

Just as the comet started to roar along so quickly that it was covered in flames, Uncle Shawn wished quietly and as strongly as a human has ever wished: "I do hope that all of my friends on the farm are safe and happy and well. I really do wish that with all my heart and ears and toes." And then he put on a very splendid purple hat and closed his eyes and wished some more.

KNEES
KNOCKING

SECTION THIRTY-SEVEN

In which we find … oh, I do hope it's nothing horrible.
In fact, I wish very hard that it's nothing horrible and
that we start to have a happy ending with everybody
safe and well and with their noses still attached.

You will remember that back on Earth, Bill and
Brian and all the llamas were in dreadful danger.
The sticky spider suit was now acting like a kind
of net and stopping Bill and Brian from moving, or helping their friends. Miranda waved her
saw and laughed and then started using it to cut
through the section of web hiding Brian's nose.

"I'll cut off the other noses while those idiotic

llamas are asleep, but I want to take your nose while you're awake!"

We can agree that's probably the nastiest thing anyone has ever said to a llama.

Brian's knees – with two remaining knee pads – were knocking together so fast that he might have been dancing the Waylas. (Of course, his knees would have been leaping with joy if he'd been dancing the special Peruvian Waylas dance, instead of having his nose threatened.) "Please not my nose, please ever so much. I need it."

Pearlyclaws sidled over (he was still scared of the spiderwebs) to try to hold Brian still while Miranda cut the web to expose the poor llama's nose. Bill was trying to kick Pearlyclaws' shins, but the web was wrapping tighter and tighter round Bill's legs and sticking in his fur. "I love you, Brian! Be brave!" Bill shouted.

"Emergencia! I love you, too!" Brian shouted.

This was terrible.

OH NO!!!!!

But then...

...

...

OH YES!!!!
FFFWWWWO
OOOOSH
THUMP.

Travelling faster than its own sound, the young comet landed straight on top of Miranda Badger and squashed her as flat as a nasty plastic bottle filled with cruelty. The comet also caught Pearlyclaws across those horrible sneaky feet that he was so proud of. It rolled them out as flat as evil pastry and it also knocked off the end of his nose.

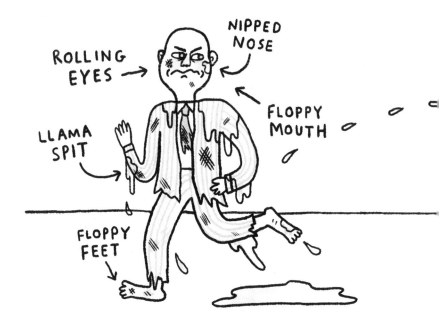

One moment things were awful and getting worse and the next there was nothing left of Miranda but a nasty big stain and a bent saw, and Pearlyclaws was flapping his pulverised feet and yowling in pain.

All this noise woke the sleeping llamas and, because they were startled and upset (and Carlos felt as if someone had kicked him), they all did exactly what upset llamas do. They took one look

at the frightening, furious face of Pearlyclaws
with its glistening head and flopping mouth and
floppier feet and nipped nose and rolling eyes ...
and they laid their ears flat along the sides of their
necks and tipped up their chins and spat great,
big, hot mouthfuls of llama spit in long fountains
all over Pearlyclaws. Some of it even went into his
open mouth.

Then Pearlyclaws gave another huge howl

– "MMWAAAAAAA! OWWWWWWWW!" – and with three pairs of llama eyes glaring at him, and Bill growling inside what was left of the spider costume, and Brian shouting, "Go away! Go away!" Pearlyclaws ran away as fast as he could manage, his floppy feet sounding like old towels soaked in badness. All his terrible plans were in ruins and he would never look good in sandals again! 🐾

LUCKY KITTEN

SECTION THIRTY-EIGHT

In which there are astronomers and a very

lucky kitten and maybe, just maybe, so much

happiness it will make your toes feel tickled.

And it could be that there are scones...

Meanwhile the young comet – now wearing Miranda's tool belt, which it thought might be useful – bounced way up high and then came down again and squashed Cedric and Lancy Bumption, who were just about to frighten a kitten. Without Uncle Shawn's wish they might have gone on being nasty to all kinds of people and cats.

Then the comet bounced even higher, pushed back upwards with wish energy, and went off into space to enjoy itself some more.

Astronomers, who had only just recovered from seeing the moon look peculiar, noticed a comet rushing upwards and shimmering with rainbow wish colours and decided they needed more than a cup of tea. Perhaps they would have cake and a short holiday, too.

Bill and Brian were almost as happy as a safe kitten. They were freed from the sticky spider threads and bits of safety equipment that had made their monster costume, all with the help of the World Association of Spiders.

After that, Brian and his three llama friends nuzzled noses so that they wouldn't be scared as Brian told them the story of how they had all nearly lost their noses. They shivered and rubbed noses again.

"Even though spitting is not ladylike, I am glad

HOLIDAYS *for* weary ASTRONOMERS

special deals

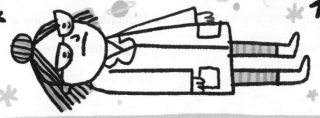

Do you feel like a LuNAR-TiC?
Has Saturn run RINGS around you?
Do you have TELESCOPE TIREDNESS?
Planets behaving a-MARS-ingly?

SPECIAL HOLIDAY HOMES WITH <u>NO</u> VIEWS OF THE NIGHT SKY

SLEEP ALL NIGHT AT LAST!

Eat custard until it all goes back to normal!

that we spat all over that terrible human being," announced Guinevere.

"He was only making my nose better so that he could cut it off!" Ginalolobrigida shuddered. "That's not what llama noses are for. They are meant to be the first beautiful bit of me that you see when I come into a room – before you notice all of the beautiful rest."

"Unless they are behind you and they see your big llama bottom." Carlos giggled. And then – because he was feeling kind – he added, "Because you have a beautiful big llama bottom."

All the llamas grinned.

"Thank you, Brian, for being such a courageous llama," whispered Ginalolobrigida. "You may be nervous sometimes, but when you have to be brave, you are like a lion – only llama-shaped."

Brian blushed almost as brightly as Wufflebuffle.

"And thank you Bill, for being also so brave. We are all very sorry that your favourite lady

badger love turned out to be as rotten as a bucket of fish guts left out in the sun for a year." Ginalolobrigida nodded sympathetically.

"She was so nasty. And I was so silly." Bill sighed. "I should have asked Uncle Shawn's advice about being in love. I hope he's OK. And Sky and Sam – they've been on the moon for ages."

All at once, all the animals said together, "I wish Uncle Shawn was here."

And do you know what? Just at that moment, the great iron soup dish glittered and spun and bounced down over the meadow where they were all standing. They only had enough time to say, "Hooray!" and "Look! Sky! We can see Sky!" and also, "We should make scones for everyone!" then the twins and Uncle Shawn were jumping out of the dish and there were lots of hugs and giggles and even some tickles while everyone explained what had happened to everyone else – sometimes all at once.

Uncle Shawn hugged Bill last of all. "I am sorry that I did not insist you should come to the moon with us. Or say that she seemed a very bad badger."

"And I am so sorry that I was a foolish fool and let so many dreadful things happen," said Bill, hugging his best friend very tight. "All the furniture has gone and there's nothing in the kitchen, not even a pinch of flour – no one can make scones! Miranda robbed us and Pearlyclaws came back and…" He stopped talking and sniffled. He felt very ashamed.

Uncle Shawn hugged him back and patted his ears and said, "Don't worry, Bill. We will find everything and put it back. It will be a chance to spring clean. But first we will go to Mrs MacMuckle's World of Scones in Pandrumdroochit and have scones and a big pot of tea, and some lemonade for all the wonderful llamas, and cakes for the twins. Look at the twins! Both of them! Aren't they wonderful?

And you, Bill, you are wonderful. I missed you so much. And..." Uncle Shawn ran to the iron dish and carried back a huge, long Uncle-Shawn-armful of amazing hats. "I brought you back some wonderful wish hats from the moon. Next time we will go to the moon together. Or maybe you can bring a lady friend. The moon is very romantic."

Bill's hair ruffled up as he said, "No romance. No romance for a long time. Nothing lovey-dovey at all – not for years and years and years. Maybe not ever." He held Uncle Shawn's hand. "But it would be lovely to go to the moon. Thank you."

"Great!" yelled Uncle Shawn. "But now ... SCONES!"

Our friends ate scones and then followed Miranda's dirty big tracks to find the cave full of their belongings and took them home again. And they opened up Miranda's secret chest and found all kinds of things in it that she had stolen from the people of Pandrumdroochit. So they had a good time working out which thing belonged to which person and then giving everything back and enjoying tea and lemonade and thank yous.

Slowly all of our friends made the farmhouse cosy again. Guinevere got back her knitting needles, and in all the barns and corners the llamas set out tiny cups of water and lemonade for any spiders who happened to be thirsty.

After only a few days, everything on the farm was back to normal, only with more hats, more powdered air for moon trips, better friends, more bravery and even more scones.

SCONES

EVEN MORE SCONES

· · ·

Then one evening Carlos and Guinevere were being friends and playing snap, Ginalolobrigida was looking at her perfect nose in her nose mirror, and Brian was lying on his straw bed watching a special performance by the Flying Teeny Weenies – a famous spider trapeze act that Claude thought he would enjoy. And they were probably the happiest llamas alive.

On the sunset side of the farm, Bill and Uncle Shawn were sitting in their rocking chairs, being as happy as they could be and then a bit more happy than that. The sun was sinking into the sea and the moon was getting brighter and, if they tried very hard, they could hear it tingling and ringing and singing with wishes.

"I'm so glad you're back, Uncle Shawn."

"And I'm so glad to be with you, Bill."

"You don't have treasure buried anywhere, do you?"

"Ha! No, I don't have any treasure. I have just enough and if I get any extra I give it to people or animals who need it more than me. I found out by accident that helping anyone who is in trouble feels even better than being tickled."

"And being tickled feels very nice."

"Of course. And hearing a joke is like being tickled in your brain and in your tummy both at once."

They both sighed contentedly and looked at the moon together.

Uncle Shawn said, "You'll like the moon people – they're very nice. They just get confused some-times. We all get confused sometimes."

He admired the big new adventure hat that Bill was wearing. Bill loved all the moon hats Uncle

Shawn brought him. Bill's old hats had been rescued from Miranda's nasty cave – all except the
pink one which he had left there to smell of soot
and mildew (along with the awful pink bow tie).
This meant that Bill had more hats than ever before
in his life. He thought he might even give some to
the llamas when they had birthdays.

"Thanks so much for the moon hats, Uncle
Shawn," said Bill. "I'm so glad that none of them
are pink."

"And thank you for being so brave while I was
away," said Uncle Shawn. "Why is six scared of
seven?" He chuckled and wriggled his fingers like
octopus feet.

"Because seven eight nine." Bill laughed. "What
do you call a flying monkey?" He giggled and wiggled his paws like squid feet.

"A hot air baboon!" Uncle Shawn wriggled his
wibbly hair. "Why don't owls fall in love when it's
raining?"

"Easy!" Bill wiggled his nose. "Because it's too wet to woo!" Then he pointed straight up at the sky. "Look! Look! Oh, I've always wanted to see one and now I have!"

Up above the two friends, a huge, old Milky Moon Moth was flying. Moon Moths are very rare – some people may even tell you that they don't exist and aren't as wide as a bus and don't have beautiful big silvery feet covered in shiny, tiny hairs.

MILKY MOON MOTH

KIND EYES

BIG SMILE

LARGE AND SOFT HAIRED FEET

LOVELY WINGS

Delighted by the rainbow sparkles of the moon way out in space, the giant moth flew loop-the-loops and then she grinned. (Or wiggled her wing tips and nodded her head – which is much the same thing as grinning for Moon Moths.) Uncle Shawn and Bill applauded and she wiggled her wings and waved her toes to them (which was a great honour) before she slowly moved away, the scales on her huge wings glimmering like lucky wishes.

The two friends cheered and tickled each other some more with jokes, and drank proper, nice cocoa, which was just as it should be.

The sun disappeared and the moon rose high in the sky with a little shadow and a little shine, which was also just as it should be. And when anyone on Earth looked up at the moon and wished, there was a chance their wish might come true. 🐾

A. L. KENNEDY

A. L. Kennedy was born in a small Scottish town far too long ago and has written books for adults and children, but mainly adults. Before that she made up stories to amuse herself. It has always surprised her that her job involves doing one of the things she loves most and she's very grateful to be a writer. She has won awards for her books in several countries. She has travelled all over the world and enjoyed it immensely. She plays the banjo badly, but makes up for this by never playing it anywhere near anyone else.

GEMMA CORRELL

Gemma Correll is a cartoonist, writer, illustrator and all-round small person. She is the author of *A Pug's Guide to Etiquette* and *Doodling for Dog People*, and the illustrator of *Pig and Pug* by Lynne Berry, *Being a Girl* by Hayley Long and *The Trials of Ruby P. Baxter* by Joanna Nadin (among other things). Her illustrations look like a five-year-old drew them because she hires one to do all her work for her. She pays him in fudge. His name is Alan.